D0012595

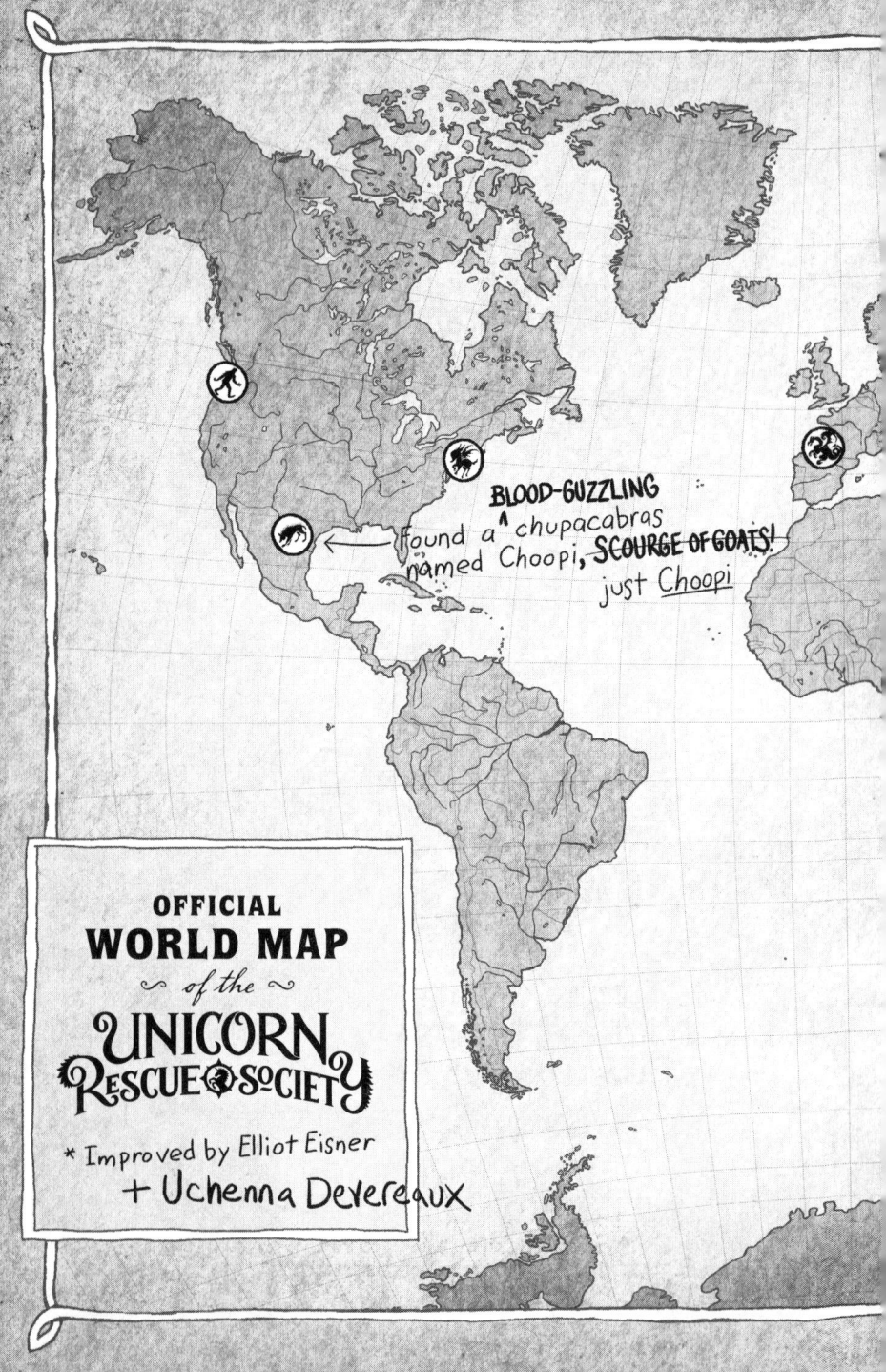

THE UNICORN RESCUE SOCIETY
THE CHUPACABRAS OF THE RÍO GRANDE

BY **Adam Gidwitz & David Bowles**

ILLUSTRATED BY **Hatem Aly**

CREATED BY **Jesse Casey, Adam Gidwitz, and Chris Lenox Smith**

PUFFIN BOOKS

*To the kids of Laredo, Texas—especially the very talented students
of The Writer's Block —A.G.*

To all my brave and loving friends on both sides of the river —D.B.

*To the little heroes of the world that go unnoticed,
you are a treasure —H.A.*

PUFFIN BOOKS

An imprint of Penguin Random House LLC, New York

First published in the United States of America by Dutton Children's Books,
an imprint of Penguin Random House LLC, 2019
Published by Puffin Books, an imprint of Penguin Random House LLC, 2020

THE LIBRARY OF CONGRESS HAS CATALOGED THE DUTTON CHILDREN'S BOOKS EDITION AS FOLLOWS:
Names: Gidwitz, Adam, author. | Bowles, David (David O.), author. | Aly, Hatem, illustrator.
Title: The chupacabras of the Río Grande / by Adam Gidwitz and David Bowles;
[illustrated by Hatem Aly] | Description: New York: Dutton Children's Books, [2019] | Series: The Unicorn Rescue Society; [4] | Summary: "Uchenna and Elliot travel with Professor Fauna to the Texas-Mexico border to save the region's animals and help bring a divided community back together with the help of locals"—Provided by publisher.
Identifiers: LCCN 2019004161 | ISBN 9780735231795 (hardback) | ISBN 9780735231801 (ebook)
Subjects: CYAC: Animals, Mythical—Fiction. | Animal rescue—Fiction. | Chupacabras—Fiction. | Friendship—Fiction. | Race relations—Fiction. | Mexican-American Border Region—Fiction. | BISAC: JUVENILE FICTION / Legends, Myths, Fables / General. | JUVENILE FICTION / Social Issues / Friendship. | JUVENILE FICTION / Historical / General. | Classification: LCC PZ7.G3588 Chu 2019 | DDC [Fic]—dc23
LC record available at https://lccn.loc.gov/2019004161

Puffin Books ISBN 9780735231818

Edited by Julie Strauss-Gabel
Design by Anna Booth • Text set in Legacy Serif ITC Std

Printed in the United States of America

1 3 5 7 9 10 8 6 4 2

UNICORNS ARE REAL.

At least, I think they are.

Dragons are definitely real. I have seen them. Chupacabras exist, too. Also Sasquatch. And mermaids—though they are *not* what you think.

But back to unicorns. When I, Professor Mito Fauna, was a young man, I lived in the foothills of Peru. One day, there were rumors in my town of a unicorn in danger, far up in the mountains. At that instant I founded the Unicorn Rescue Society—I was the only member—and set off to save the unicorn. When I finally located it, though, I saw that it was *not* a unicorn, but rather a qarqacha, the legendary two-headed llama of the Andes. I was very slightly disappointed. I rescued it anyway. Of course.

Now, many years later, there are members of the Unicorn Rescue Society all around the world. We are sworn to protect all the creatures of myth and legend. Including unicorns! If we ever find them! Which I'm sure we will!

But our enemies are powerful and ruthless, and we are in desperate need of help. Help from someone brave and kind and curious, and brave. (Yes, I said "brave" twice. It's important.)

Will you help us? Will you risk your very *life* to protect the world's mythical creatures?

Will you join the Unicorn Rescue Society?

I hope so. The creatures need you.

Defende Fabulosa! Protege Mythica!

Prof. Mito Fauna

Mito Fauna, DVM, PhD, EdD, etc.

CHAPTER ONE

It was a peaceful morning in Miss Vole's classroom.

Miss Vole was giving a lecture about the Mexican-American War.

Every student was absolutely silent. Not because they were mesmerized by Miss Vole's lecture. They were absolutely silent because pretty much every single student was fast asleep.

Pai Lu had her head on her desk, her eyes

were shut, and she was rhythmically breathing through her black-lipstick-covered lips.

Janey was bent backward over her chair, her mouth wide-open, as if she were dead.

Jasper and Johnna were leaning against each other, Jasper's head nestled in the crook of Johnna's neck. They were gently snoring in harmony, like two blenders of different sizes, running at the same time.

Jimmy was doubled over on himself, his head between his knees.

Uchenna sat directly behind Jimmy. She was awake, because Jimmy kept silently farting in his sleep. She wanted to poke him and tell him to stop farting, but every time she reached out her finger to poke him, another fart wafted in her direction, making her curl up in a ball and whimper.

Elliot was also awake. He was furiously taking notes on Miss Vole's lecture. He was pretty sure that some portion of it would be on the test. If there was a test. Which Miss Vole had never mentioned. But he wanted to be ready. Just in case.

"In the year 1836," Miss Vole was saying, "more than one hundred and eighty years ago, Texas and California were a part of Mexico's territories. Have you heard of *Texas* and *California*, children?" Miss Vole always talked to the class like they were kindergartners. It drove Elliot crazy. And, apparently, it put everyone else to sleep. "*Texas* and *California* are *states*. In the *United States*. But they didn't use to be! You see—"

BOOM!

Every kid in Miss Vole's classroom sat straight up.

Janey snapped forward and hit her head on the table.

Pai Lu said, "Werewolves?! Zombies?! Vampires!? What's happening!?" And then she said, "Please let it be vampires!"

Jasper and Johnna pulled away from each other, disgusted that they'd been cuddling without realizing it. And then they each took a breath. They spun around in their seats and faced Jimmy. "Ugh!" Johnna moaned. "What did you *eat* this morning?!"

Jimmy sat up and grinned.

Then they all turned to the source of the booming sound.

The classroom door had been thrown open. Standing in the doorway was a tall, thin man in a tattered tweed suit. He had hair like a tidal wave, a beard streaked with black and white, and eyebrows you could lose a pen in.

"*Perdón*, Miss Vole," said Professor Fauna, the most eccentric social studies teacher on the planet—and the founder of the secret Unicorn Rescue Society. "I need Uchenna and Elliot. Right away."

Miss Vole looked unhappy. "Professor Fauna, you're *always* taking those two. They have missed *far* too much class already. Whatever you're taking them for, it can't *possibly* be—"

"It is *very* important, Miss Vole. I need them to watch television with me."

Miss Vole squinted. "What?"

All the kids stared at Professor Fauna. Elliot and Uchenna included.

"Yes!" Suddenly, Professor Fauna seemed less confident. "Uh . . . you see . . . television is very important! There is much information that can be gathered from TV! You can watch the news, the sports, the weather, the fake news, the fake sports, the fake weather. *Muy importante.*"

"Can I come?" Jimmy asked. "I want to watch TV!"

The professor looked at Jimmy. "What? In school? Are you kidding? TV rots your brains! Besides, you look like you watch too much TV already. Try reading a book, young man. Elliot and Uchenna, *¡vámonos!*"

And he left the room.

Elliot and Uchenna quickly collected their backpacks and walked to the classroom door. Elliot turned back to the class and waved sheepishly before following Professor Fauna down the hall.

Miss Vole shook her head, as if waking up from a dream, and then turned back to the class. "Where was I? Oh yes! Did you know that California and Texas are *states*?"

Twenty children instantly fell asleep.

CHAPTER TWO

Uchenna and Elliot hurried to keep up with the long strides of the professor. He swept down a staircase, and then down another one, and they followed, until they were in the subbasement of the school. As they strode past large, humming air-conditioning units and yellow buckets on wheels with mop handles sticking out, Elliot tried to ascertain just what was going on.

"Do you really want us to watch TV with you, Professor?" Elliot asked, practically running to keep up. "I mean, while TV is safer than trying to rescue a dragon or a sasquatch, I'm not sure we should be missing *class* for it."

Professor Fauna stopped in front of a door with five dead bolts running down one side. The sign on the door read janitorial supplies. But pasted over that was a piece of paper that said, MITO FAUNA, DVM, PHD, EDD, SOCIAL STUDIES DEPARTMENT. "You do not understand, Elliot," Professor Fauna said as he unlocked the dead bolts, one by one. "On the TV is something about—"

"A mythical creature that needs our help?" Uchenna blurted out.

Professor Fauna nodded. "At least, so I believe."

He pushed the door open and revealed a tiny office, no bigger than a mattress, lined floor to ceiling with bookshelves. Against one wall was a small desk, and above that was a series of maps and charts with crazy scribbles all over them. Professor Fauna walked to a bookshelf and pushed some books to one side, revealing a tiny television. He turned it on. A tiny black-and-white picture appeared. On the screen, a barrel-chested man with a giant cowboy hat was talking to a reporter. The words BOB BRAUNFELS, RANCHER ran across the bottom. There was no sound, though. Professor Fauna fiddled with a knob on the little TV. Suddenly, they could hear it.

". . . drained of blood. All of it," the rancher was saying. "I've never seen anything like that in my whole dern life. A young cow—just lyin' there, dead."

The reporter said, "Sounds like a vampire bat, Mr. Braunfels."

The rancher stared dismissively at the reporter. "Vampire bats are smaller than my hand and can't drink more than an ounce of blood. Whatever this was took a couple *gallons*."

"And you saw two holes in its hind leg, just above the hoof?" the reporter asked, pushing the microphone closer to the rancher's face.

"No, not two. *Three.* Three puncture wounds. Like a huge rattler bit it on one side—and then half bit it again on the other side. Strangest dern thing. Also, rattlers put poison *in*. They don't take blood *out*. No idea what could have done it. Must have come across the border."

"You think the culprit came into Texas from Mexico?" the reporter asked.

The cattle rancher pushed his big hat back on his head. "Well, I've never seen nothing like this on our side of the Río Grande, so I reckon it must have. Who *knows* what they've got over there!"

The reporter shivered as she turned to the

camera. "Well, this has been a live report from Laredo, Texas. Stay tuned to this channel for—"

Professor Fauna switched off the TV. "You see!?"

"See what?" Elliot asked. He looked genuinely afraid.

"What could do something like that?" Uchenna asked. She also looked scared. Which was unusual for her.

Professor Fauna said, "The bite pattern is right, but it shouldn't behave in that manner! Unless there is something very, very wrong with it. It may be sick. Or crazed. Or rabid. Or—"

"*What* might be sick or crazed or rabid?" Elliot demanded.

"What? Oh! A chupacabras, of course!"

"A what?" said Elliot. "A *choo-puh-CAH-brahs*?"

Uchenna cocked her head at Elliot. "You don't know what a chupacabra is? Is it possible that there's a mythical creature that I've heard of, that you haven't?"

Elliot pursed his lips. "It seems that there might

be, though I am perturbed by the notion. I *am* still waiting for *Deadly Beasts of Kazakhstan* to be returned to the public library. Maybe it's in there . . . ?"

"The chupacabra is a bloodsucking monster!" Uchenna announced, shuddering. Then she smiled a little, which perturbed Elliot even more.

Elliot turned to the professor. "She's exaggerating, isn't she? She's just trying to scare me."

Professor Fauna shrugged. "Technically, she is right. Except she is saying it wrong. It is *chupacabras,* both singular and plural. The name means 'sucker of goats.' You are saying 'sucker of goat,' which sounds very weird."

"Uh, they *both* sound weird," Uchenna clarified.

Professor Fauna considered this. After a moment, he said, "Yes, I suppose that is true. Now, come! I will tell you more in the airplane!"

"What?! It *is* a bloodsucking monster?" cried Elliot. "Also, if we *have* to go anywhere near that thing, do we have to take the *Phoenix*?" The *Phoenix* was the Unicorn Rescue Society's single-propeller airplane, which crashed every single time they flew it. Somehow, Professor Fauna always got it working again.

"Elliot, it is a thirty-hour drive to Laredo from here. We must fly! *¡Hay que apurarnos!*"

"Wait!" Uchenna exclaimed. "Where's Jersey?"

"Already in the *Phoenix*! *¡Vámonos!*"

Professor Fauna dashed out of the office door. Uchenna was hard on his heels. Elliot watched them go.

"Doesn't anyone think we should just stay in school today?" he asked.

No one answered because he was all alone, in a tiny janitorial closet that doubled as the world headquarters of the Unicorn Rescue Society. He threw up his hands and followed the professor and Uchenna to the airplane, which would take them to Texas (if it didn't crash), where they would encounter a bloodsucking monster.

Elliot sighed. "This is the worst extra-curricular activity ever."

CHAPTER THREE

Moments later they were in the parking lot, boarding the battered blue-and-white plane. Uchenna helped pull Elliot up into the *Phoenix*.

As Elliot strapped himself in, he said, "So, tell me more about this creature I've somehow never heard of."

Uchenna said, "Well, a chupacabras is short and has spines down its back. It looks a lot like a bald coyote crossed with a porcupine. It hops on its hind legs, kinda like a kangaroo. Oh, and it has sharp, long teeth. Like needles. The chupaca-bras plunges them into a victim's flesh and . . ." She trailed off as she noticed Elliot turning green.

Professor Fauna clambered into the cabin and started jabbing at the plane's controls with his calloused fingers. He squinted at the dials. "Truly, we know very little about the chupacabras. It has been ignored not only by science, but also by scholars of mythology. Information about it has mostly survived as urban legends, passed among schoolchildren and through popular culture, like television programs and viral videos and—"

Elliot stopped him. "Wait. Do I not know about this creature because I don't hang out enough with other kids? I'm spending too much time reading books or something?"

There was a long, awkward pause. Professor Fauna stared at Elliot, unblinking, his bushy eye-brows beetling together. Uchenna looked at the rusty floor of the *Phoenix*.

Elliot sighed.

Professor Fauna continued. "At any rate, there are journalists in Mexico who have taken reports of chupacabras more seriously. Reading their newspaper articles and doing my own research, I have come to a number of conclusions about them. For example, I believe that chupacabras travel in packs."

Elliot said, "You want us to fly to Texas and face a horde of bouncing vampire coyotes? Are you kidding?"

"There is no cause for concern," Professor Fauna replied. "Chupacabras are only known to latch on to the ankles of *animals* and suck the blood from their bodies. No human has ever been attacked."

"*That we know of,*" Uchenna whispered dramatically.

Just then, Elliot felt something sharp grab his ankle.

"AHHHH!" he screamed.

A blue blur rose into the air in front of him. Two red wings came beating up into his face.

"AHHHH!"

"Elliot! Relax! It's just Jersey!" Uchenna was laughing.

Jersey settled in Elliot's lap and looked up at him, blinking his big yellow eyes. Elliot exhaled and stroked the soft fur on Jersey's head.

The plane suddenly roared to life. The doors locked with a loud click. They began to taxi down the school parking lot toward the street.

"*¡Nos vamos a Texas, vaqueros!*" shouted Professor Fauna over the roar of the engine. Then, in a horrible Western accent, he repeated himself in the language of cowboys from old TV shows: "Vamoose, buckaroos!"

Elliot settled back with a sigh, strapping himself in again. The *Phoenix* picked up speed as it reached the end of the lot, but the professor didn't yank back on the yoke to lift it into the air. He was busy fiddling with the dials of the radio.

"We need to find the perfect music, *amigos míos*!" he exclaimed.

"Excuse me?" Uchenna said, indignant. "When did you get a radio in this plane?!"

"It seems our Muckleshoot friends at the Boeing plant installed it.* Now, to face the chupacabras, we must get into the right mood."

Elliot's eyes went wide as he looked through the cockpit window. He pointed, terrified.

Dozens of cars were moving slowly through the school zone.

The plane was going to drive right into the traffic.

---

* See *The Unicorn Rescue Society: Sasquatch and the Muckleshoot*

"Professor!" Elliot shouted. "Pull up!"

Suddenly, a song began blasting from the speakers: trumpets, guitars, violins, and emotional singing in Spanish.

"Mariachi!" Uchenna shouted. "I love mariachi music!"

Then, just as they were about to plow into the passing cars, Professor Fauna yanked back hard on the yoke, and they rose above the street, their wheels almost grazing the top of a city bus.

The *Phoenix* shuddered under the strain. Elliot thought he might pass out.

The professor and Uchenna didn't seem to care. They were singing together, in unison with the radio:

"*¡México, lindo y querido!*"

As the trumpets crowed and the guitar was strummed dramatically, Elliot stroked Jersey and sighed.

They were going to Texas. All the way down to the border.

CHAPTER FOUR

Uchenna looked out the window at misty green peaks below them.

"Those are the Appalachian Mountains, aren't they?"

"Yes," Professor Fauna said. "We are making very good time."

Elliot was pretty sure they were making unrealistically good time, but he decided to change the subject back to mythical creatures. "So, what else do we need to know about chupacabras?"

"Well," Professor Fauna replied, "the word first appears in 1995, in Puerto Rico. Over the course of a few months, sheep and goats were found dead, drained of blood, in the town of Canóvanas."

Elliot brightened at this grisly news. "Oh! No wonder I hadn't heard of them. They're pretty new!"

"In truth, Elliot," Professor Fauna said, "these creatures have, like all animals, been around for millions of years. But the name *chupacabras* is new. Twenty years before they were identified in Canóvanas, the Puerto Rican town of Moca lost much livestock to a being the residents called *el vampiro de Moca.*"

"The Moco vampire?" Uchenna tried translating. She had started attempting to pick up a little Spanish from Professor Fauna, since they were spending so much time together.

"Close, but not quite. *Moca,* not *moco. Moco* means 'booger.' The booger vampire would not be very scary. And the chupacabras is closely tied to what people fear. After the 1995 incident, people throughout Latin America began reporting similar attacks. But in most cases, there were no chupacabras. When people are afraid, they give their fear a name. Sometimes, you are afraid of something and you don't know why, or it is too complicated to talk about. So, you come up with another cause of your fear. You might be afraid of hunger, or crime, of your society changing, or even of the government. But you call your fear *el chupacabras*."

"Wait," Elliot said. "Are you telling us chupacabras are *not* real?"

"No! I only mean that many of these reports are not true. For example, I am certain that chupacabras do not *kill* their prey when they suck their blood. If they did, many more animals would be dead, and the chupacabras would have been hunted to near extinction, like the wolf. My guess is that they are much more like a vampire bat: Their prey would have to be asleep and would likely not even know when they woke up that the chupacabras had been there."

"But you said sheep and goats were found dead," Uchenna objected. "And that rancher dude's cow was definitely dead."

"Ah yes," said Professor Fauna. "This is confusing to me. This is why we must go to Laredo to investigate."

"Because now chupacabras seem to be *killing* things," Elliot clarified. "Yeah, that sounds like a *perfect* time to go check them out."

Elliot stared out the window and reconsidered every choice he'd made in his life that had brought him to this moment. Jersey crawled into his backpack to sleep, and Uchenna pulled out a smartphone.

"When did you get a phone?" Elliot asked.

"My birthday," she told him. "I bugged my mom and dad. Told them it would be perfect for doing research online. Which is what I'm doing now."

"Research into what?"

"Laredo. Listen to this. It sounds like Laredo, Texas, has got a pretty interesting history. It was founded as part of New Spain. When Mexico gained its independence, Laredo rebelled and became the capital of the Republic of the Río Grande."

"I've never heard of the Republic of the Río Grande," said Elliot.

"That's because it only existed for one year," said Uchenna. "The Mexican military retook it. But then in the Mexican-American War, the United States took Laredo—and all of Texas and California, too."

"Texas and California are *states*," Elliot informed her.

Uchenna laughed. "Yeah, but they used to be part of Mexico."

Professor Fauna tapped some buttons and turned some dials that didn't seem to do anything. "Yes, children. For one hundred and fifty years, Texas, California, Nevada, Utah, and most of the Southwest have been part of the United States. For the thirty years before that, they were part of Mexico. For three hundred years before that, they were claimed by Spain, though many had never even *heard* of Spain! The people along the Río Grande lived like they had for six *thousand* years, members of Coahuiltecan nations like the Carrizos and Comecrudos. But for that land and those tribes, the borders and rulers keep changing."

"That sounds confusing," said Elliot.

"Yes," agreed Professor Fauna. "When an army shows up and tells you you're suddenly in a different country, even though you haven't moved at all, it can be very confusing indeed."

"Check this out," Uchenna said. "After Laredo became part of the United States, the people of Laredo asked the United States government if they could rejoin Mexico. When the US refused, many of them moved across the Río Grande and founded the city of Nuevo Laredo, on the other side of the border. Now they are sister cities. Families have members on both sides."

"Wow," said Elliot. "Can they visit each other?"

Professor Fauna answered. "It used to be easier to go back and forth. Now everyone must have the right papers and status and so on. Some officials on the US side want even more separation than just the river and the border patrol. Look out the window. We are almost there."

CHAPTER FIVE

Uchenna peered over Elliot, out the window of the *Phoenix*. In front of them, a broad river snaked its way between two sprawling cities. "Laredo," Elliot said, pointing out the city to the north.

"And Nuevo Laredo," Uchenna said, pointing out the city to the south.

Professor Fauna crawled out of his seat and started rummaging on the floor behind it. Without him at the controls, the *Phoenix* began to pitch and yaw, up and down, back and forth.

Uchenna quickly unstrapped herself and slid behind the steering column to keep the plane steady.

"You know you don't have a license," Elliot scolded her.

"I'm not sure he does, either," Uchenna shot back as she struggled with the yoke.

"*¡Los encontré!*" the professor shouted, brandishing a pair of binoculars. "My young friends, look more closely."

Elliot took the binoculars and peered

through them toward the river. On the southern side, Nuevo Laredo was built right up to the wide waterway, which marked the border between the United States and Mexico. But on the northern side, the city of Laredo was set back, with some low trees and chaparral between the buildings and the water's edge.

"So, is there a fence or a wall or anything?" Elliot asked, scouring the banks of the river for some sort of boundary between the two countries.

"Well, for many years the only barrier was water—that river you see—which we call the Río Grande," Professor Fauna said. "But in some places, they have built a fence. Look over there."

Elliot followed his outstretched finger to what looked like a college campus on the American side. There, a tall, black, wrought-iron fence, with sharp, curved spikes at the top, ran alongside the scrubby desert.

"And now," said Professor Fauna, "look there."

Uchenna saw it first, even without binoculars. She gave the airplane's controls back to the professor, tapped Elliot on the shoulder, and said, "There."

Next to one stretch of the wrought-iron fence, huge machines had torn great holes in the earth. Part of the fence had been ripped down, and towering slabs of concrete replaced it, casting a long shadow over the dry ground.

"They're building a border wall," she said quietly.

"*Así es.* Correct." Professor Fauna began to circle the *Phoenix* away from the river. "We should not land nearby. It would draw too much attention. I think that highway, just outside Laredo, makes better sense."

Elliot double-checked his seat belt and got a firm grip on the backpack. Landing was not one of Professor Fauna's strengths.

The professor pushed forward on the yoke. The plane dropped toward the blacktop below.

Elliot closed his eyes, gritted his teeth, and dug his fingers into the armrest of his seat.

A minute later, the *Phoenix* settled onto the highway with the slightest of jolts, its motor sighing softly as it shut off. The brakes engaged gradually and smoothly.

Elliot opened his eyes in shock. They were rolling to a stop. Nothing bad had happened.

"What?!" exclaimed Uchenna. She looked out the window, slightly disappointed. "No plowing through the creosote? No smashing through cactuses?"

Elliot coughed. "Cacti."

Just then, a metallic groan shuddered throughout the *Phoenix,* and both its wings fell off onto the asphalt.

"Yes!" Uchenna shouted.

Elliot shook his head, his mouth suddenly dry. "What if they'd fallen off when we were flying over the Appalachians? We would be so dead right now."

In response, Professor Fauna spun a dial on the radio until the voice of a DJ came blaring out in a mix of English and Spanish.

"*Chequen sus cabras* and cows, folks! Get them in the shade *si no están muertos.* It's gonna be a hot one *aquí en* Laredo today!"

"Ah, Tex-Mex," the professor said with a smile. "Welcome to the border, my friends!"

CHAPTER SIX

Cars zoomed by the *Phoenix* as it rattled its way, wingless, down the two-lane highway. The air was hot and dry—the kind of hot and dry that makes you want to sit on your front porch and drink soda from a glass bottle. Jersey clambered out of his backpack to look out the windows. The fields around them were filled with sagebrush and stubby acacia trees. Black, shiny birds swooped from low branches to the edges of the highway, looking for trash to peck at.

"Look at that desert," said Elliot, as the heat rose in shimmery waves from the dry, shrubby ground.

"This is the chaparral," Professor Fauna said. "Not quite desert, but close."

Uchenna pointed at the shiny black birds. "Those are the weirdest crows I've ever seen."

"Not crows. Grackles," Professor Fauna replied. "You should hear the noise they make. They sound like an old radio. Speaking of radios, listen to this classic *norteño* tune!"

A swaying melody came from the *Phoenix*'s small speakers. Accordion, guitar strummed lightly with the fingertips, an acoustic bass.

"It's a little corny," said Elliot.

"Yeah," Uchenna replied. "And I love it."

"You love this *and* you love heavy metal?" Elliot asked, incredulous.

"And rap and country music and gospel and—"

"I get it! You like music."

"No," said Uchenna, fixing him with a stare, "I *love* music." Then she turned up the volume, so the walking bass line and the squeeze of the accordion filled the hot little plane. And Uchenna started to make up words to go along with the instrumental tune:

> *Oh, here we go*
> *To Old Laredo,*
> *Capital of the Río Grande.*
> *Just watch your step,*
> *Or the sucker of goats*
> *Will suck blood from your hand.*
> *Or your foot.*
> *Or your neck.*
> *Or your face.*
> *Or your—*

"Uchenna!" Elliot said.

Uchenna grinned and shrugged. "Sorry."

HONNNNNNNK!

A deafening horn blast made Professor Fauna swerve onto the shoulder of the little highway, spitting up rocks from the *Phoenix*'s three wheels. Jersey squealed and dove back into his backpack. With a *whoosh* of air, a giant truck came barreling past. The tiny, wingless airplane shuddered and swerved in the draft of air that the truck created.

"*¡Qué barbaridad!* That man is driving like a maniac!" cried Professor Fauna, trying to keep

the plane steady on the narrow shoulder of the two-lane highway.

HONNNNNNNK!

Another eighteen-wheeler came roaring past. The walls of the tiny plane shook. This truck was identical to the first, with a shiny black cab and a long silver trailer. Dust billowed in its wake, coating the windshield of the *Phoenix*.

Professor Fauna swerved back and forth, trying to see through the cloud of dust.

HONNNNNNNK!

"*¡Palabrota!*" the professor shouted. "What is this, a tractor-trailer convention?!"

A third giant semi with a shiny black cab and a silver body came thundering by. Elliot stuck his head against the side window. "Look!" he called.

"I wish I could!" Professor Fauna shouted back, trying to peer through the dust-coated windshield. "I can see nothing!"

CRUNNNCH!

All the passengers of the *Phoenix* were thrown forward against the controls console—except Jersey, who was plastered onto the windshield. The little plane shuddered to a halt.

"For example," said Uchenna, "you didn't see the ditch you just drove into?"

The plane's front right wheel was wedged in a drainage ditch that ran along the side of the highway.

"Precisely," said Professor Fauna. "I did not see that."

Elliot threw open the door of the little airplane and hopped out. "Quick, look!"

Uchenna and the professor clambered from the plane as quickly as they could. They followed the direction of Elliot's outstretched finger.

Their expressions became as hard as the dirt of the desert.

"I should have known," Professor Fauna muttered.

"Yup," said Uchenna. "Of course."

"Those," Elliot said, gesturing at the snake-like *S* on the back of the semi that was rumbling away in a cloud of dust, "are Schmoke Industries trucks."

CHAPTER SEVEN

"But what are the Schmoke brothers doing down here?" asked Uchenna. "Do you think they came when they saw the TV report about the chupacabras?"

Professor Fauna said, "Perhaps. But then why did they bring three enormous trucks? What sinister scheme requires that kind of hardware?"

"I'm sure we'll find out soon enough." Elliot shuddered.

Just then, they saw a little blue shape bound

out of the airplane. The bright sun of South Texas lit up Jersey like a set of gemstones—a lapis-lazuli body with two ruby wings. He bounded across the hard-packed dirt, between sage-green bushes and stubby mesquite trees. The grackles croaked at him.

"They *do* sound like old radios," said Uchenna. "Like they've got static in their voices. And they look like someone spilled oil on their backs."

Jersey crouched in front of a grackle and growled at it, deep in his little throat. The bird flew away. But Jersey kept growling at . . . at nothing, it appeared.

"Uh, what's he doing?" asked Uchenna.

Suddenly, Jersey bounded off into the chaparral. "Wait!" Uchenna called. "Jersey!"

"He is probably chasing a jackrabbit," said Professor Fauna.

"Oh. That's okay," said Elliot.

"Or maybe a rattlesnake," the professor added.

"What?! Jersey!" Elliot called. "Jersey, stop!"

Elliot ran a few steps after Jersey, then thought about the rattlesnake and stopped, then decided that it was worth risking his life for Jersey, and then tripped and stumbled directly into a barrel cactus. "YEOWW!" he shrieked.

Elliot walked back to the professor and Uchenna, clutching his arm. Long spines stuck out of his skin like acupuncture needles. As the professor helped Elliot pluck them out, Jersey came trotting up beside them.

"What were you after, little guy?" Uchenna asked, picking him up and rubbing his furry blue head. He looked at her proudly, as if he'd chased off a great and terrible danger, and they should all be thankful to him. "Weirdo," said Uchenna, and she rubbed his head some more.

"There!" Professor Fauna said as he plucked the last cactus spine from Elliot's arm. "Now, back to the car!"

"It's a plane, Professor," Uchenna said.

"Yes, but we are *using* it as a car." They walked back through the scrub to the *Phoenix*, Uchenna cradling Jersey like a baby, Elliot rubbing his arm and grimacing. "Tell me, children," the professor went on, "is the *Phoenix* defined by its intention, or by its function? It was made to be a plane. But we are *using* it as a car. So which is it? Or, as another example, if you have a book, but you use it to level the legs of your sofa, is it really a book? Or is it a sofa-leveler? Is there a word for this in English? A sofa-leveler?"

Elliot scanned his internal mental dictionary. "Uh, I don't think so."

"I don't think there is one in Spanish, either," Professor Fauna said. "Anywhat . . . So, what is this sofa-book? Is it its intention, or its function? Or take this border wall that is being built. What is it *intended* to do? Enforce the immigration laws of the United States, no? And what is it *actually* doing? Maybe enforcing the laws, but also dividing communities and families who have always lived on both sides of the border. So what *is* the wall? This is a question a philosopher might answer by—"

"Professor," said Elliot.

"Yes?"

"Don't we have to find some chupacabras, stop them from sucking the blood from all the cattle in Texas, figure out what the Schmokes are up to, and still get home before dinnertime?"

"Ah, right. Okay. The TV report said there would be a meeting at the Laredo city hall about the dead cows," said Professor Fauna. "I think we should begin our searching there." They all climbed into the *Phoenix*. "On the drive, though, let me tell you what the philosopher Elizabeth Anscombe has to say about intention and function. . . ."

Within moments, Uchenna, Elliot, and Jersey were all fast asleep. The professor, on the other hand, delivered a fascinating lecture to the *norteño* band on the radio.

CHAPTER EIGHT

"*Despierten, chibolos*. We have arrived."

Uchenna shook herself awake. The professor had squeezed the *Phoenix* into a parking lot across the street from a large, multistoried building that had to be Laredo City Hall. A crowd of people had gathered outside, some of them carrying homemade signs and shouting slogans.

"Come on, Elliot," Uchenna said, tapping her friend on the shoulder. He jerked open his eyes with a start. "What? Where? Oh. Laredo. Suckers of goats. Yay." He rubbed his eyes, then yawned as he unbuckled his harness and grabbed the backpack. Jersey was still asleep inside.

The members of the Unicorn Rescue Society exited the plane and crossed the narrow street. Uchenna wiped sweat from her forehead. "It sure is hot."

Professor Fauna nodded. "Yes, and it is still morning. Wait until the afternoon."

As they weaved their way through the noisy crowd outside city hall, they realized the people had all gathered to protest—but for *different* protests. Some people held signs that read PROTECT OUR CATTLE FROM RUSTLERS or BUILD THAT WALL, while others proclaimed TODOS UN PUEBLO—WE ARE ONE PEOPLE and STOP SEPARATING FAMILIES. A few groups of protestors were shouting at one another, but most were calmly chanting their slogans or handing out brochures.

"Wow," said Elliot. "The chupacabras attack really got people riled up."

"I think they're upset about more than that," Uchenna replied, eyeing the crowd warily.

They passed a looming statue of George Washington and made it through the tall double doors of the modern city hall. The high-ceilinged atrium just inside was glowing with light from the big windows above the door. The broad space was full of people, many milling about the receptionist's desk.

The professor led Elliot and Uchenna down a hall to the council chambers, where a meeting was in session. The doors were open, but all the seats were taken. People were standing behind the chairs and along the walls, tightly packed together.

At the front, the city council members sat behind a high bench. Before them was a podium. A woman was addressing them. Her brown hair bounced up and down as she slapped her hand against the podium.

"Listen to yourselves! It's ridiculous to think

people are crossing the border just to kill our cattle. Shame on everybody who's using the death of a cow as an excuse to support building a border wall!"

"That voice," muttered Professor Fauna, squinting and standing on tiptoes to see over the crowd. "Why is it so familiar?"

Just then, a tall man nearby wearing a broad-brimmed cowboy hat shook his head, muttered something, and walked out of the council chambers.

"The rancher!" exclaimed the professor. "Mr. Braunfels, from the television! I need to speak with him!"

Pulling anxiously on his unruly hair, the professor hurried after the man.

"What about us?" Uchenna shouted after him.

"Investigate, children. Question others. Find out what you can," he called back over his shoulder.

Elliot fanned his face. "Can we investigate outside? These angry people are using up all the oxygen."

Uchenna nodded. "Let's go."

CHAPTER NINE

Elliot and Uchenna managed to squeeze back through the crowd and out of the building, to the public square under the bright blue sky. A few yards away, the professor had cornered the rancher and was moving his hands about in exaggerated gestures. They heard Bob Braunfels say, "Are you *serious*?" And then, "That's why we need a wall!"

Elliot stopped. "What do you think the professor is saying?" he asked Uchenna. "He's not telling the rancher about the chupacabras, is he?"

Uchenna shrugged. "I doubt it. Would the rancher even believe him if he did?" She began looking around for someone to interrogate. She noticed a couple of kids standing under the twisting branches of a live oak.

"Let's talk to them," she said. "They can't be nearly as crazy as all these shouting grown-ups."

Elliot and Uchenna walked toward the two kids—a boy and a girl, possibly siblings—about the same age as Uchenna and Elliot. The boy was holding a Styrofoam cup in one hand, spooning some sort of red snack into his mouth.

"Hey," said Uchenna, as they approached.

The girl pushed her long, black hair behind one ear. "Hey," she said. She looked from Uchenna to Elliot and back again. "Are you here to protest the wall, or support it?"

Elliot and Uchenna glanced at each other. What was the right answer? After a pause, Elliot decided that the best answer, as usual, was the truth:

"Neither. We're looking into something else."

Now it was the boy's and the girl's turn to glance at each other. The girl said, "That sounds mysterious." The boy put some more red stuff into his mouth, without taking his eyes off Elliot.

Uchenna said, "What do you know about the way that calf died?"

The girl said, "Blood sucked out of it. Everyone knows that."

Elliot decided to stay cagey. "What could have done that?" he asked.

The boy and the girl made eye contact again. The girl said, "What do *you* think did it?"

"Oh, we've heard some crazy stories," Uchenna told her breezily. "Vampires . . . enormous leeches . . ." She paused. "Chupacabras."

The boy had brought the spoon up to his mouth, but at this he lowered it. "Chupacabras, huh?"

"There might be some evidence." Uchenna shrugged.

"What evidence?" the girl replied, a little too quickly. Then she tried to look like she didn't care.

Elliot was *terrible* at pretending that he didn't care. "What evidence?!" he exclaimed. "How about the three tooth marks—two on top of the ankle and one underneath!"

The boy and the girl looked very serious now. "How do you know so much about chupacabras?" asked the girl.

Uchenna said, "Who says we do?"

But Elliot, at the exact same moment, said, "We're part of a society." As soon as it was out of his mouth, he wanted to kick himself. The Unicorn Rescue Society was *secret*. There were too many people who might want to hurt the animals of myth and legend. Or, just as bad, take advantage of them.

But now the boy and the girl both looked very tense. They were leaning forward with interest. The boy said, "What kind of society 'looks into' chupacabras?"

Elliot knew he had said too much. He looked at Uchenna. Still trying as hard as she could to play it cool, she shrugged and said, "Why do you care?"

The boy and the girl communicated without a word. They were so in sync they *must* have been brother and sister. After a moment, the brother said, "Let's just say we care about keeping chupacabras safe from those who might misunderstand them."

This impressed both Uchenna and Elliot. They looked at each other, tried to communicate as subtly as these two kids did, realized they couldn't, and so at last Elliot nodded.

Uchenna turned back to the brother and sister. "Our group is called the Unicorn Rescue Society."

Neither Elliot nor Uchenna was prepared for the looks of amazement on the siblings' faces. The girl's jaw dropped open. The boy nearly choked on his snack.

The girl pounded the boy on the back to make sure he wasn't *actually* choking, and then turned to Elliot and Uchenna. Timidly, she said, *"Defende Fabulosa?"*

Now it was Uchenna's and Elliot's turn to be shocked.

Uchenna managed to respond, *"Protege Mythica."*

The four children stared at one another.

CHAPTER TEN

The boy said, "I'm Mateo. This is my sister, Guadalupe. We call her Lupita. Are you really members of the Unicorn Rescue Society? We have been waiting *forever* to meet one of you guys!"

"I'm Uchenna and this is Elliot," Uchenna replied. Then she cocked her head at Mateo and Lupita. "So . . . wait. Are you members of the Unicorn Rescue Society, too?"

Lupita shook her head. "No. We wish. One

day, we were snooping around our mother's office at home—"

"Don't judge," Mateo interjected around a bite of his snack, which never seemed to run out. "She's a biologist, and her office is full of super-cool stuff."

"Anyway," Lupita continued, "we found an old scientific journal locked away in her desk. One of those things that science organizations publish once a year. *Procedimientos de la sociedad para el rescate de los unicornios.* That's Spanish. It means—"

"*Proceedings of the Unicorn Rescue Society*?" Uchenna said.

Elliot scratched his head. "We have a scientific journal? What the heck? When was Professor Fauna going to tell me? I could be the editor!"

Lupita took a sharp breath. "Dr. *Mito* Fauna? DVM, PhD, EdD?"

Uchenna nodded. "Yup. He's our mentor in the Unicorn Rescue Society. He's over there somewhere, talking to a witness. You know him?"

"He wrote most of the articles in the *Proceedings*, so, yeah!" Lupita said excitedly. "He's a genius."

Uchenna started laughing. "Oh yeah, definitely. A mad genius."

Elliot squinted against the sun, which was nearly above them now and hotter than ever. "So, your mom's a biologist. Did you ask her how she got the journal?"

"She doesn't know we've read it," Mateo said, waving his plastic spoon back and forth, like looking at her private stuff would be a big no-no. "She can be kinda secretive."

Elliot peered at the cup. "What *are* you eating, Mateo?"

"Watermelon with chili powder." He spooned some up and held it out to Elliot. "Want some?"

Who in their right mind ruins watermelon with chili powder? Elliot wondered. If this was an indication of border cuisine, he sure hoped they got back to New Jersey by dinnertime. But he just replied, "Uh, no thanks. I'm, uh, not into spicy food."

Lupita pointed to the entrance to city hall. "Look! There's our parents. Mom must've finished talking."

Mateo added under his breath, "Or they threw her out."

Grabbing Uchenna's hand, Lupita gestured at the boys. "Come on. You've got to meet them. They are *so* going to be surprised!"

Mateo shook his head and tossed his cup into a nearby trash can before muttering to Elliot: "We are *so* going to be in trouble. Lupita's going to try to be all clever when she mentions the Unicorn Rescue Society, but she'll put her foot in it. I better help."

Mateo and Lupita's parents greeted them with warm smiles as Lupita approached, Uchenna in tow. Their mother was tall, with long brown hair, dark eyes, and a hazelnut complexion. She was the

woman Elliot and Uchenna had seen speaking in the chamber. Their father was a little shorter, black hair contrasting with his lighter eyes and skin.

"Mamá, Dad! How did it go?"

"Ay, *m'ija*, they just won't listen." Her mother shook her head. "I see you made new friends, though."

Lupita smiled. "Oh yes. Now, before I introduce them, I need to explain something."

Mateo arrived beside his sister, with Elliot behind him, and announced: "We broke into your office last year and read about the Unicorn Rescue Society. These two guys are members."

"Mateo!" Lupita exclaimed, her cheery demeanor disappearing. "A little more finesse, no?"

"Better to just rip the Band-Aid off."

Their mother had narrowed her eyes. Her gaze was furious.

"*¿Cómo pudieron?* I strictly asked you—"

"Mamá," Lupita said sweetly. "We were wrong, and we know there will be consequences. But right now? Please, listen. Elliot, Uchenna, this is my mom, Dr. Alejandra Cervantes, and my dad, Israel Cervantes."

Uchenna reached out her hand. "Hi, Dr. Cervantes. Nice to meet you. We're here about the chupacabras."

The woman shook Uchenna's hand. "I don't understand. Where are you from? If you're really with the society, what chapter?"

Elliot cleared his throat. "Well, I guess the original one. We're students of Professor Fauna's."

Mr. Cervantes did a double-take, staring at his wife in shock. "Wait. Fauna's here? Did you contact him?"

"What?" she said, mortified. "No!"

Uchenna could sense the tension, so she interrupted to clarify. "We saw the reports on TV. We flew down so the professor could interview some rancher dude."

Scanning the crowd, Elliot caught sight of Fauna's unmistakable hair. "There he is now, by the statue of George Washington."

Her face scrunching up strangely, Dr. Cervantes stormed off in that direction. Her husband hurried after, trailed by Lupita and Uchenna.

"Oh, man," muttered Mateo. "This is gonna be good. Sensing some majorly messed-up vibes right now."

As they all hurried after Dr. Cervantes, the backpack on Elliot's back began to move, jerking and twisting on his back. Jersey was awake and wanted out.

"*Not now!*" Elliot hissed over his shoulder. "Totally the wrong time, little guy!"

"Uh, Elliot?" Mateo said. "Are you talking to your backpack?"

"It's complicated. I'll explain later."

Professor Fauna was just shaking hands with the rancher when Dr. Cervantes reached him. She barked: "*¿Qué haces aquí, Erasmo?* Don't you have any creatures to harass in Lima?"

The professor whirled around, his eyes wide.

"Alejandra?" he asked, dumbfounded. "What are *you* doing here?"

CHAPTER ELEVEN

"Why aren't you in Mexico?" demanded Professor Fauna.

"Why aren't *you* in *Peru*?" Dr. Cervantes demanded right back.

Professor Fauna regained his composure a little. "I live in this country now. Teaching young people and continuing the work. And you?"

Dr. Cervantes eyed him and then allowed her anger to subside for a moment. "Same here. I finished my doctorate. I came to Laredo to teach at

Texas A&M International University. And I met Israel. A wonderful herbalist. Not a bad husband, either." Israel wiggled his fingers at the professor and gave a goofy grin. "Now we have these two brilliant *huercos*," she went on, "who can't seem to stay out of their mother's private files." Dr. Cervantes ended this statement with a glare at Mateo and Lupita. They both looked at their shoelaces.

"But . . ." Fauna beetled his bushy brows. "Who is keeping watch over the *gente pájaro* down in Monterrey?"

Elliot felt Jersey slam against his back, frantically trying to escape. Pulling the backpack off his back and gripping it reassuringly against his chest, Elliot unzipped it a little and peered inside. Jersey was invisible.

"*Shhh,*" Elliot whispered into the backpack.

Gente pájaro. Uchenna tried to decipher that with her rudimentary Spanish. "Uh, 'bird people'? Is that a thing?"

Dr. Cervantes smiled. "Yes, Uchenna, though

they're really more like spider monkeys with wings and a bad attitude. That's how I met your teacher, you see. I was a biology student in the city of Monterrey—that's in Mexico—when he came barging into my life, recruiting me into the Unicorn Rescue Society so I could help him save these little, flying simian creatures. Oh, I was as excited as you must be, going on adventures, risking life and limb. *Defende Fabulosa! Protege Mythica!* But then I woke up."

Elliot glanced up from the backpack. He'd been too distracted by Jersey to follow the conversation closely. "On his plane? I bet it was during a landing. He can't quite . . . you know, *land*."

Professor Fauna scoffed. "Bah. More like you *gave* up, Alejandra. Children, you are looking at the only individual to ever formally renounce her membership to the Unicorn Rescue Society."

Dr. Cervantes let out a loud laugh. "Ha! Yes, it was the ethical thing to do."

The sound of her guffaw startled Jersey. He became visible and poked his snout out of the backpack, growling. Elliot tried to push Jersey's blue head back inside. Jersey snapped at the boy's finger with a frustrated snarl.

"What is that?" Lupita demanded.

Elliot sighed, glanced around to make sure no strangers were looking, and let Jersey's head poke up out of the backpack. The little blue creature sniffed the air.

"And that!" Dr. Cervantes said, shaking her head in disbelief. "That is exactly what I mean! You brought a . . . What *is* that?"

Professor Fauna suddenly looked abashed. "A juvenile Jersey Devil," he muttered.

"A juvenile Jersey Devil! You brought it to Texas, sealed up inside a backpack?! That creature should be in New Jersey, in the wild, studied at a distance by qualified scientists! They should not be treated like a pet!"

Professor Fauna sighed heavily. "Again with this? They need us!"

"They need us to leave them alone. The URS system? Conscripting well-meaning but misinformed adults and children to care for these legendary species? It is wrong. All interference with animals and their natural habitats is wrong. I have been studying the chupacabras here for years—but always from a distance!"

Mr. Cervantes mumbled, "Such a distance you've never actually seen one . . ." Dr. Cervantes shot her husband a withering look.

"Alejandra," Professor Fauna went on, "if humans put these creatures in danger, then it is our responsibility to help them!"

"And," Uchenna said, pointing to the backpack, "just so everyone's clear, we didn't *mean* to keep Jersey as a pet. If he had wanted to stay in the Pine Barrens, we would have been happy for him. *He* adopted *us*."

At the sound of her voice, Jersey raised his

upper body completely out of the backpack and licked Uchenna's outstretched hand.

Dr. Cervantes shrugged. "So you say. But did you *feed* him?"

Uchenna and Elliot looked at each other and then at the pavement beneath their feet.

Lupita made a frustrated whine. "Mamá, you said last night that we needed to protect the chupacabras. Well, these folks want to help. It's what they do."

"Amigos," Mr. Cervantes murmured, "careful."

He pointed his forehead at people mulling around the square. Several were staring at Jersey, pointing and muttering to one another. Elliot guided Jersey back into the darkness of the backpack. "Why don't we continue this conversation over lunch?" suggested Mr. Cervantes. *"En casa de la familia Cervantes."*

"Good idea," Dr. Cervantes said. "Is your car nearby, Professor?"

"The *Phoenix* is across the street, in the parking lot."

"You flew to city hall?"

Elliot shook his head. "No, ma'am. He drove it like a car from the outskirts of town. The wings fell off after landing."

Dr. Cervantes couldn't help but laugh. *"Ah, qué hombre este.* It figures. Well, follow us, then. Hopefully you won't get stopped. Laredo police aren't used to ratty old planes on their streets, wings or no wings."

CHAPTER TWELVE

A n hour later, they were relaxing around a rough-hewn, rustic table in the Cervantes family's bright and colorful kitchen. Elliot was surprised at how much he had enjoyed the food Mr. Cervantes served them. No chili-dusted fruit on the menu at all, just piles of tightly rolled and fried chicken tacos called flautas, accompanied by a zesty salad, black beans, and the most delicious guacamole he had ever tasted.

Apparently, Professor Fauna agreed with this

assessment, as several times during the meal the professor had seized the large stone mortar that held the guacamole and served himself heaping spoonfuls.

Sipping on his *agua de melón*—a refreshing drink of cantaloupe blended with water and honey—Elliot tried to gain some clarity on the problem at hand. "Okay, so I'm confused. It sounds like chupacabras just showed up thirty years ago. But that's not biologically possible. Professor Fauna, you said something about them being much older, right?"

Mateo waved a flauta back and forth. "Yah, they just got *that* name recently. They've been around for a long time. Dad knows all about them. He runs a *hierbería*—like an herbalist shop, but with traditional folk medicine from Mexico and stuff. He's a *curandero*."

Lupita jumped in. "Yeah, Mamá may be the scientist in the family, but Dad's got all the ancient indigenous knowledge. Best folk healer in Laredo."

Mr. Cervantes ruffled her hair with a smile. "*Ya*. Not quite, *m'ija*. But it's true that I have access to older traditions. So, I know that chupacabras have been around for a very long time, well before the Conquista, the Spanish conquest of Mesoamerica."

"What's Mesoamerica?" Uchenna asked.

Elliot said, "Mesoamerica means, you know, Mexico and Central America. Before Columbus and Cortés."

"Exactly," Mr. Cervantes continued. "For example, Mesoamerican mythology speaks of a beast called the Tozcoyotl: yellow-feathered coyote."

"Those I've heard of!" Elliot exclaimed, wheels turning in his head as he began to put the chupacabras in a historical context. "Could those feathers be like chupacabras quills?"

TOZCOYOTL

Dr. Cervantes grinned and gave him a thumbs-up. "You nailed it, Elliot. I've studied a few quills we've managed to collect from old warrens—chupacabras make their lairs underground—and they share many characteristics with feathers."

"But that's not the only evidence," Mr. Cervantes continued. "The local Carrizo tribes spoke of the *glam pakua'm* or 'biting beast.' The Aztecs drew images of a spiny-backed creature known as the *ahuizotl*, nicknamed *ezzoh* or 'blood-thirsty thing.'"

AHUIZOTL

"Wow. So there's a long history of these vampires?" Uchenna said. "Draining people's blood all over Mesoamerica?"

Elliot felt his stomach churn. "Maybe death by blood-draining isn't the best topic for lunch conversation."

"Oh, the chupacabras doesn't normally drain its prey," Dr. Cervantes clarified, putting

a reassuring hand on Elliot's shoulder. "Like a vampire bat, it drinks a little blood from a sleeping animal, without killing it. However—"

A scraping noise stopped her midsentence. Professor Fauna was using his spoon to get every last bit of guacamole from the stone mortar. He noticed the others staring at him, and he set the bowl down sheepishly.

"*Perdón.* Your guacamole is truly spectacular, Israel."

"*Gracias, Profesor.* I can make more if you like." Mr. Cervantes half rose from his seat.

"No, no. *Qué va.* I have had more than enough." Elliot could tell from the obsessed look in Fauna's eyes that this wasn't completely true. "You were saying, Alejandra?"

"Well, perhaps if something disturbs a pack's feeding pattern, the chupacabras might go into a frenzy, draining too much blood. It's just a theory, of course."

"What sort of things could disturb their feeding pattern?" Uchenna asked.

"A disruption in their lifestyles, I would guess," Dr. Cervantes replied.

"Like hunters?" Mateo asked.

"Highways?" suggested Uchenna.

"Radiation from cell phones?" Elliot added.

Suddenly, the conversation was interrupted by strange, wet, slurping sounds. Everyone turned to look at Professor Fauna.

He was licking the guacamole bowl, streaks of green smearing his beard.

Dr. Cervantes snapped at him, "Erasmo!"

Professor Fauna looked up, half crazed. After a couple of seconds, his eyes refocused, and he blushed.

"My apologies," he said, and gingerly put down the bowl.

Uchenna was shocked, not by her teacher's behavior (which she had learned to roll with), but by his name.

"That's the second time she's called you 'Erasmo.' I thought you were *Mito* Fauna."

Dr. Cervantes laughed. "Oh, he is, dear. *Mito* is a nickname for 'Erasmo.'"

Lupita made sharp gestures in the air with her hands, as if showing the evolution of the word. "Yeah. Erasmo. Erasmito. Mito."

Uchenna and Elliot both looked shocked.

Mateo gave a small chuckle. "Dude. You actually thought his parents named him 'myth,' right?"

Elliot shrugged. "If they're as weird as he is . . ."

Professor Fauna said, "Enough about me. How shall we help these creatures before this overzealous community captures them . . . or does something even worse?"

CHAPTER THIRTEEN

As Dr. and Mr. Cervantes, Professor Fauna, Elliot, Uchenna, Mateo, and Lupita sat around the table, Jersey began to sniff around the glossy clay tiles of the floor. First, he appeared to be searching for food scraps from their lunch—which he found plenty of under Professor Fauna's chair. He gobbled them up hungrily.

But then it became clear that Jersey was looking for more than just a snack. He sniffed his way over to a corner where a small niche had been built into the wall to hold a statue of a woman in flowing robes.

Uchenna noticed what Jersey was doing. "What's that statue Jersey's sniffing?" she asked quietly, as the adults continued discussing the chupacabras problem.

"Oh," Lupita replied, "we're Catholics. That's our *nicho*, with the Virgin Mary."

"Dad calls her Tonantzin," added Mateo. "She watches over us."

Jersey was sniffing his way over to a long, low table, covered with a frilly cloth and set with photographs and candles. Rising up the wall behind the table were more photographs. They all seemed to be of the same person.

"And what's he sniffing now?" Elliot asked, leaning over to join Uchenna and Lupita's conversation.

Mateo answered, "That's our altar to our *abuela*, Concepción."

"We called her Mamá Conchita," Lupita added wistfully. "She was the family matriarch."

Jersey was now wandering through an open doorway, sniffing the ground . . . the corners . . . the air . . .

"What's with him?" Elliot asked.

"Dunno," Uchenna replied. "What's in that room, Lupita? Is he allowed to go in?"

"That's my mom's office. Maybe we should go get him," Lupita replied. "*Apparently*, my mom doesn't like people snooping around in there." She looked at Mateo and they both shrugged guiltily.

Lupita turned to her mother to ask to be excused from

the table—when a loud *CRASH* erupted from Dr. Cervantes's office.

"¡Dios mío! ¿Qué pasa?" Dr. Cervantes cried. The four kids were already up on their feet and sprinting toward the office. *CRASH! SMASH!* It sounded like Jersey was taking a hammer to a chandelier.

When they made it to the office, they saw that Jersey was scrabbling at a tall cabinet. The room was full of glass jars holding animal specimens— stuffed opossum and mice and hawk feathers and jackrabbit skulls. But at least three jars were lying on the floor, cracked or shattered. And as Jersey tried to leap up the side of the cabinet again, beating his wings to gain altitude, he knocked into another jar, which sent both him and the jar tumbling toward the glossy brick floor.

Uchenna ran and slid, pushing broken glass out of her way with her extended foot, like a baseball player sliding into home plate. The jar fell directly into Uchenna's arms.

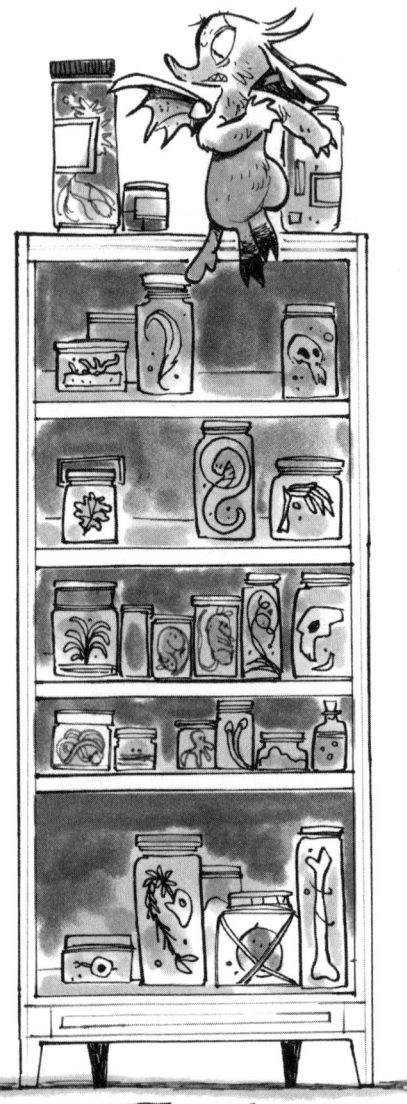

"Wow!" Mateo cried. "That was awesome!"

Unfortunately, the jar had fallen into Uchenna's arms upside down, and dozens of brown pellets spilled all over her.

"Uh, what is this stuff?" she asked, holding a brown pellet between her fingers.

"Uh, that would be spoor," Lupita answered.

"Better known as poop," Mateo added.

Uchenna dropped the pellet and scrambled to her feet, frantically brushing the pellets off of her.

Jersey was trying to climb his way up the cabinet again. Elliot grabbed him before he could smash anything else. Jersey fought against Elliot's grip.

"What has gotten into him?" Professor Fauna asked. The adults had arrived at the doorway of Dr. Cervantes's office and were surveying the destruction.

"This is what happens when you keep a wild animal in captivity!" Dr. Cervantes scolded them. "Their instincts—"

Suddenly, Jersey got free and launched himself from Elliot's arms into the air. His wings lifted him up on top of the cabinet. There, he attached himself to a rough wooden box and started gnawing at it.

"Let me guess," said Professor Fauna. "You keep almond bars in that box."

"He is obsessed with almond bars," Elliot agreed.

"It is going to bankrupt me," the professor added. "And the nice lady at the grocery store thinks I have a problem."

"That's not a box of almond bars!" said Dr. Cervantes. She pushed a chair over to the cabinet and climbed up on it. "Look!" She picked up the box—which was about the size of a toaster—and, with Jersey still clinging to it, passed it to her husband. Mr. Cervantes put the box down on a desk. Jersey was still gnawing on it.

"Please take hold of your captive wild animal," Dr. Cervantes said.

Uchenna grabbed Jersey and pulled him away from the box. Dr. Cervantes removed the carved lid and pulled out a strange object. It was long and yellow and looked like a cross between a porcupine quill and an eagle's feather.

"Is that . . . ?" Elliot murmured.

"It is," said Dr. Cervantes. "A single barb of a chupacabras."

Jersey strained at Uchenna's grip, trying to get at it.

"What's with Jersey and the chupacabras spine?" Lupita asked. "It's like he's obsessed with it or something."

Elliot reached out for the chupacabras barb. "May I?" he asked. Dr. Cervantes nodded. Elliot gingerly took the spine from Dr. Cervantes. Jersey followed its path like his nose was iron and it was a super magnet. "Maybe," Elliot said, waving it slowly in front of Jersey, "*this* is what he smelled out on the highway when he went running into the desert."

"Where did your captive wild animal run into the desert?" Dr. Cervantes asked.

"Highway 359," Elliot answered, as Uchenna glared at her.

Lupita looked at him incredulously. "You know 359? Have you been to Laredo before?"

"There was a *sign*," Elliot said, as if everyone remembered every street sign they ever saw.

Dr. Cervantes was getting excited. "The grazing territory out by Highway 359 is where I have long suspected chupacabras activity! But I could never find them!"

Elliot waved the barb back and forth, back and forth. Jersey's eyes followed it like a metronome. "Well, now," Elliot said, "we have a bloodhound."

CHAPTER FOURTEEN

D r. and Mr. Cervantes climbed into their minivan, which was beige with a sparkly sheen.
But Mateo and Lupita hesitated.

"Can't we all ride in the *Phoenix?*" Mateo
asked, jerking his thumb at the wingless plane.

Dr. Cervantes glared at her children. "Listen,
we may be running around with Erasmo, but—"

Professor Fauna interrupted her, "I am afraid
that for our current project, the anonymity of a
minivan better suits our purposes."

"Anonymity?" Mr. Cervantes objected. He ran his hand over the hood of the minivan in an exaggerated gesture. "My ride is the color of *champagne . . .*"

As Lupita walked past her father and got into the minivan, she said, *"Ay, Papá, eres un gran perdedor."*

"I am not a loser!" her dad said. "I am just enthusiastic about *this ride . . .*" He started doing the hand gestures over the hood again. Lupita buried her face in her hands. Everyone else laughed.

Soon, they were standing on the side of the highway 359, looking out across a flat land of sagebrush and tiny, twisted trees. Heat rose from the dirt in visible waves.

Jersey was in his backpack on Uchenna's stomach, scrabbling to get out.

"So," said Professor Fauna. "We let him out. And he runs. And we run after him. And we see what happens. Yes? This is the plan?"

"Not as scientific as I would like," Dr. Cervantes muttered.

"You have a better one, dear?" Mr. Cervantes asked, wiping sweat from his forehead.

She shook her head and squinted at the desert.

"Just to be clear," said Elliot. "We are going to be running through the desert, where there are rattlesnakes and probably scorpions—"

"Definitely scorpions," clarified Mr. Cervantes.

"Okay, rattlesnakes and *definitely* scorpions, trying to locate a pack of spiny, bloodsucking monsters?"

Dr. Cervantes nodded and kept staring at the desert. "That's about the size of things."

Elliot asked, "Would this be an appropriate moment to say *Dios mío*?"

Lupita grinned. "Yup."

"Ready everyone?" Uchenna asked. "Here goes nothing."

She unzipped Jersey's backpack. He launched himself from it and went scampering across the dusty ground, zigzagging this way and that, following his snuffling nose. Suddenly, he seemed to catch the scent, and he went galloping off through the chaparral. The whole team went running after him. Jersey ran, and then leaped and glided for a few moments, and then ran again.

"Fan out!" Mr. Cervantes called, as they fell further behind. "We're less likely to lose sight of him that way!"

So they fanned out, jogging through the heat, trying to follow Jersey's zigzags through the desert.

The hot afternoon sun blazed down on them. Elliot wiped his forehead with his bare forearm—only to realize he was transferring more sweat to his brow than he was taking off.

Uchenna slowed. "What is that?" she called to her friends. Up ahead, a wide band of chaparral seemed to be . . . *shimmering*.

At the same moment, Elliot shouted, "Guys, I think I'm starting to hallucinate. I'm seeing a lake! In the desert!"

"It *is* a lake," Lupita called back.

Mr. Cervantes was standing at the lake's edge, gesturing to them all. "*¡Vengan!*" he was saying. "*¡De prisa!* I think Jersey has found something!"

CHAPTER FIFTEEN

A snarling sound came from the reedy bank. Mr. Cervantes gestured at everyone as they ran up. "Quickly! Make a semicircle right here! If Jersey has found the chupacabras, we'll grab him."

"With our bare hands?" Elliot exclaimed. "It has *spines*, right?!"

"Grab him by the legs," Mr. Cervantes suggested. "Or the belly. Oh, and watch the teeth, too."

"*Madness*," Elliot muttered to himself.

At just that instant, Jersey yelped in surprise,

and a bright flash of yellow exploded from the dense reeds and then froze.

Everyone took a collective breath of surprise.

A creature crouched in front of them, its little head swiveling slowly to look at each person in turn, golden eyes turning red as they reflected the noontime sunlight.

It resembled a small, hairless dog. Its skin was mottled with different shades of light brown. Its knobby spine ended in a short tail, tufted yellow like the quills that ran like a Mohawk over its head and down its neck.

The creature dug into the dirt with raccoon-like paws, each digit tipped with a black claw, and hissed at them, baring three long, needle-like fangs—two pointing downward from the top of its mouth, and one up. Drops of saliva oozed down them.

"*Okay,*" whispered Dr. Cervantes. "*No one make any sudden—*"

Which is when Jersey came flying out of the reeds, straight at the vampire dog.

CHAPTER SIXTEEN

Many things happened at once.

Dr. Cervantes grabbed Jersey straight out of the air.

Professor Fauna leaped toward the chupacabras and missed, sprawling in the dirt.

Uchenna rolled toward the creature with an expert tumble, but her sweaty fingers slipped over its hairless skin.

The Cervantes siblings were both running toward it from opposite directions, hoping to trap it, but the quilled creature started zigzagging like crazy. Brother and sister collided and dropped to the ground.

"*Lupita!*" Mateo shouted.

"*Mateo!*" Lupita shouted at the same moment.

The chupacabras rushed back toward the little lake.

Right at Elliot.

He crouched, his heart racing. Once, his uncle Alter had tried to teach him baseball. It had been a disaster, but Elliot had learned one thing—how to field a grounder. He bent his knees and lowered his hands, cupping them together . . .

And the chupacabras ran right between his legs, bounced into the air, and dove into the water.

Elliot looked up. Mr. Cervantes was hurtling toward him. Elliot fell flat on his back as Mr. Cervantes hurled himself over Elliot and into the lake after the chupacabras.

Everyone gathered at the bank, watching the ripples die down. Bubbles streamed up to the surface.

"It's okay," Mateo told Uchenna with a nudge. "My dad can hold his breath a long time."

As if on cue, Israel Cervantes broke the surface of the shallow lake and stood, water streaming from him, a wriggling bundle clutched in his arms.

"*Te tengo, cachorrito,*" he muttered, giving a fierce smile as he examined the chupacabras closely. Then he looked up at the rest of them. "Got him."

Dr. Cervantes handed Jersey off to Elliot and hurried over to examine the chupacabras as Mr. Cervantes waded out of the lake. Professor Fauna was right behind her. The hairless creature had stopped squirming and was now glaring at his

captor, eyes narrowed, as he made a low, whistling sound.

Dr. Cervantes exhaled heavily. "A chupacabras. *Cara a cara*, at last." As she marveled at the hairless little creature, its low whistling grew more intense. "Yes," she muttered, almost to herself, "this is definitely an immature male. Quills are soft and short. Paws are smaller than the tracks we've found before. But there's no sign of a pack. *Hmm . . .*"

"Perhaps he was separated from the others," Professor Fauna suggested. "It might explain why he is out during the day."

"Wait," said Uchenna. "What do you mean he's immature?"

"I find that *most* males are immature," Lupita added.

Mateo said, "Hey!"

But Dr. Cervantes was shaking her head as she ran a hand over the chupacabras's wet and trembling skin. "To say that he is immature means that he is young. A child."

"Awww!" said Uchenna and Lupita at once.

"Awww?" Elliot exclaimed. "How can you say 'Awww' about *that*?" He gestured with one arm at the hairless, spiny, mottled, golden-eyed chupacabras. In his other arm, Jersey had fallen very still.

"It's a *baby*!" Lupita cooed.

"It's not a baby, Lupita," her mother corrected her. "It's a juvenile. Probably not much older than you, in chupacabras years."

"He's just a cute little pup!" Lupita said.

Uchenna asked Dr. Cervantes, "Can I touch him?"

Dr. Cervantes looked from Uchenna to Professor Fauna to Uchenna. "Under normal circumstances, I would say absolutely not. But nothing about today is normal, so . . . Just watch out for the spines."

So Uchenna reached out her hand. Mr. Cervantes was holding the chupacabras's head, so he couldn't snap at any of them. As Uchenna stroked his side, he seemed to relax a little. But he continued to whistle through his nose, low and intense.

Lupita announced, "I say we call him Choopi!"

Uchenna nodded as she kept stroking his side. "Yeah, that works. I like it."

Elliot did a double-take. "Wait, what?" He gestured at the blue Jersey Devil in his arms. "When I wanted to name Jersey 'Jersey,' you said it was a dumb name. You wanted to name him

Bonechewer! Now we've literally caught a blood-sucker and you're fine with 'Choopi?' Gah!"

Mateo laughed. "Girls, Elliot. They stick together."

"For the record," Elliot said, "I like the name Choopi. I'm just pointing out the irony."

Professor Fauna had crouched down so that he was at eye level with the little creature. "Choopi, el chupacabras. *Buenos días, amiguito.* Now, I have a question for you. Where is your family?"

Which is when Elliot screamed, "What's happening to Jersey?!"

CHAPTER SEVENTEEN

Everyone turned to see Jersey totally rigid in Elliot's arms. It was like he'd been stuffed by a taxidermist. Professor Fauna and Uchenna rushed to Elliot's side.

The professor felt the Jersey Devil's flank. "He is still breathing. But he seems to be in suspended animation! A strange combination of a coma and rigor mortis!"

"Don't say *mortis*!" Elliot exclaimed. "It means dead!"

"He's not dead," said Uchenna. "But what's—"

And then something changed. They could feel it in the air, somehow. And then Jersey shook his red wings and began twisting in Elliot's arms again.

Professor Fauna, Uchenna, and Elliot all looked around, trying to find the source of the sudden atmospheric alteration. Their gazes came to rest on Mr. Cervantes. He was gently holding the chupacabras's nostrils closed.

"The whistling," said Mr. Cervantes. "It seems to have a hypnotic effect on Jersey."

"This must be how a chupacabras can drain

the blood from a bull!" Dr. Cervantes said excitedly. "They have the power of hypnosis!"

"Not on us though, weirdly," said Mateo.

"Maybe just on animals?" his sister added.

Professor Fauna stroked his beard. "Our large brains may be less susceptible to suggestion . . ."

"Don't call Jersey's brain small!" Uchenna said. Jersey reached out and licked Uchenna's face. She giggled and pushed him away.

"So, we don't know where his family is?" Mateo asked. He began stroking the chupacabras's head. The little creature didn't seem to mind. Since Mr. Cervantes was still holding its nose closed, it was breathing through its mouth, its tongue lolling out like a dog's. Except that its tongue was black.

"It's very strange," said Dr. Cervantes. "We know that chupacabras are pack animals. To have a young one separated from his family is unheard of. And dangerous. For him and for the livestock that live around here. Typically, juveniles don't know how to feed properly without their parents' guidance."

"What? I can eat without you around, Mamá!" Lupita objected.

Mr. Cervantes raised an eyebrow. "Oh yeah, *m'ija*? If you had all the money you wanted and lived by yourself, what would you eat for every single meal?"

Lupita paused. "Pepperoni pizza."

Mr. Cervantes nodded. "Yes. Yes, you would."

"I see your point," Lupita said.

Mateo was staring at the little chupacabras. "Man, if Choopi doesn't know where his family is, that would be terrible. I've got a pal named Andrés at school. He was born here, but his parents weren't. They've been taken to some detention center—no one knows where. Andrés is living with Mrs. Braunfels, our principal, until they can find his parents. Man, that kid is crying like every day."

They all turned back to the chupacabras, their faces twisted with sympathy.

"Are you like Andrés?" Lupita asked. "Separated from your family? How can we help you, little Choopi?"

Choopi had begun to wriggle violently in Mr. Cervantes's arms. "I think we must admit the possibility—" Mr. Cervantes said, "that he doesn't want—" The chupacabras twisted, poking Mr. Cervantes with his spines. This elicited a yell from Mr. Cervantes. He also loosened his grip.

And with that, the chupacabras was down on the ground and sprinting across the chaparral again.

"Our help." Mr. Cervantes sighed, rubbing the spot where the chupacabras had poked him.

Jersey leaped from Elliot's arms and ran after the chupacabras.

"I guess we're gonna chase them again?" Elliot asked unhappily.

Dr. Cervantes pointed after Choopi. "If the chupacabras keeps going in that direction, he'll lead Jersey straight into the *pulga*. The flea market."

Dr. Cervantes winced. "Big space. Tons of people."

"Ah," said the professor. "A chupacabras and a Jersey Devil running around a flea market. This does not sound good."

"We've gotta stop them," Uchenna said. "Grown-ups, can you drive to the *pulga*? You might get there faster. And we can text you if Choopi changes direction or if anything else happens."

Dr. Cervantes said, "That is an excellent idea."

Mr. Cervantes and Uchenna exchanged numbers, and then the adults ran toward the Cervanteses' minivan while Mateo, Lupita, and Uchenna started sprinting after the chupacabras and Jersey.

Elliot first looked after the adults, and then after the kids. "Can I say that we look like amateurs right now?" he shouted. "Why are all the adults staying together, and leaving the kids all alone? That's completely irresponsible! And what will we do when we find him? We have no plan!" No one answered. "It's, like, total amateur hour over here!" he shouted. The sound of his voice died over the chaparral.

And then more quietly, Elliot added, "I could just stand here and keep talking to myself. Or . . ." He sighed and then started jogging after Choopi, Jersey, and the other kids.

CHAPTER EIGHTEEN

Choopi took them on a brutal pursuit through chaparral, copses of mesquite, and shadeless stretches of weedy dust.

As they ran, Choopi occasionally let out a long, plaintive whistling sound. Elliot expected this to cause Jersey to freeze and tumble into the dirt, suddenly hypnotized. But it didn't. As he listened to the repeated, whining whistle, he realized that it sounded quite different from the whistle that had hypnotized Jersey.

"Uchenna!" Elliot called ahead of him, panting as he ran. "I think Choopi . . . has different kinds . . . of whistles . . . Maybe I can . . . document them . . ."

But Uchenna was nearly out of earshot, and it seemed, right then, that no one really wanted to document anything. So Elliot focused on running.

They cleared a clump of acacia and anacua trees, and the parking lot of the flea market appeared ahead of them. Choopi was dashing from car to car, hiding under one before scurrying to the next.

Jersey scampered across the blacktop. Whenever he passed through the shade of a parked car, he'd become invisible. Then he'd enter the bright sunlight again and his blue fur and red wings would sparkle.

"We can't let them enter the market," Uchenna said between gasps of breath. "Too many witnesses."

Mateo agreed. "And too many hiding places."

Right then, Choopi leaped from the hood of a car toward a tree that stood by a fence. It would take him no time at all to climb the low branches and get into the flea market.

"Oh no!" cried Lupita.

But midway through the air, Choopi suddenly dropped like a stone and began to roll around in the shade on the ground, hissing in frustration. He rolled into a sunny spot—and Jersey became visible, wrestling with the little chupacabras, trying to pin him down. But then a low

whistling sound pierced the air, and Jersey froze. Choopi wriggled free of the frozen Jersey Devil's grip and, still whistling through his nostrils, bounced from the asphalt to the lowest branch, from the branch to the fence, and then scrabbled over the top.

"That was the hypnotic whistle!" Elliot announced.

"Uh, you think?" answered Lupita, as Uchenna ran to Jersey and scooped him up. The little blue creature was shaking himself awake. Before he could wriggle free, Uchenna slipped him into the ventilated backpack and zipped it closed.

They all stood for a moment in the blazingly bright parking lot, sweaty and panting like thirsty dogs.

Uchenna's phone buzzed. She took it out. "The adults are already inside. They came in the south entrance." She punched in a reply. "Let's go in. We'll search from the north, they'll search from the south."

Elliot looked through the fence at the lines of stalls and throngs of people. "It'll be like finding a needle in a haystack," he said.

"Yeah," Lupita replied. "If a needle ran like a jackrabbit and could suck your blood."

CHAPTER NINETEEN

The *pulga* was thronging with people, all of them visiting busy stalls in the partial shade from corrugated aluminum roofs. There were stalls selling plush blankets with bright illustrations on them, stalls crammed with tables of miscellaneous electrical equipment, stalls with sneakers, and stalls with beautiful pieces of desert wood, carved and polished until they shone. Several different songs blared loudly from multiple sources, in totally different styles.

"Where could he be?" Lupita asked as they scanned the crowd.

"Just about anywhere . . . ," Elliot muttered, his senses overwhelmed by the thrumming *pulga*.

Just then, crashing sounds and screams broke through the teeming crowd and music.

"I'm going to take a wild guess and say . . . that way!" Mateo pointed in the direction of the screams. And off the kids ran.

A dozen karaoke machines and a flat-screen TV had been knocked off a display. The vendor

was shouting in Spanish and waving his hands in the air.

"What is he saying?" Elliot asked Lupita.

"I am definitely not allowed to repeat *any* of those words," Lupita told him.

"There!" cried Uchenna.

They saw Choopi scrambling over a table covered with ladies' blouses. Shoppers were recoiling in disgust and fear. The chupacabras leaped from the table and slammed into an *elote* cart, knocking it over. Corncobs and kernels and cream and liquid chili went spraying all over the asphalt.

"What?!" cried Mateo in disgust. "That's the best *elote* in Laredo!" A tiny kid started picking corn kernels off the ground and putting them in her mouth. "See?" said Mateo.

Choopi scrambled into a stand that displayed cell phone accessories. He leaped up onto a shelf, sending phone cases cascading to the ground. The elderly woman who tended the stall shrieked and threw a charger at him. It got caught in his quills. He snarled and went climbing up onto the corrugated roof. From inside the backpack, Jersey was scrabbling and fighting to get out.

"This is a disaster," said Lupita.

"We've got to catch him! For his sake!" Uchenna cried.

"And so he doesn't destroy any more delicious food!" Mateo added.

They followed Choopi from below as he leaped from roof to roof. Finally, though, he came to a place where the music was loudest and there were no roofs nearby.

Uchenna dropped her gaze and saw dozens of couples dancing. There was a live band on a little makeshift stage playing bouncy, up-tempo music.

"What in the world?" Elliot exclaimed.

"It's a *pista de baile*," Lupita told him. "A dance floor. They're playing *cumbias*. Really fun to dance to."

"In *this* heat?"

"Oh, it's always hot. We still dance," Mateo said.

Uchenna caught sight of Choopi weaving between the legs of dancing couples. None of them seemed to notice him. As the other kids surrounded the *pista de baile*, Uchenna dashed onto it. Moving to the *cumbia* beat, she tried to follow the chupacabras. But he darted off the dance floor and into a crowd of people who were sorting through piles of used clothes.

Uchenna followed, scanning left to right, up and down. Nothing.

In seconds, everyone joined her.

"We lost him," she said.

The others stared around them. Dancers. Shoppers. Vendors. Music and shouting and laughing. The smells of food and sweat and dust. But no chupacabras.

Elliot knelt down in the dirt. "What're we gonna do?" He was breathing heavily from the pursuit. He put Jersey's backpack on the ground. Jersey strained to get out.

Uchenna shook her head. "I dunno."

Lupita was watching the *cumbia* dancers. But they didn't make her feel happy, like they usually did. She was seeing them, but she was thinking of a chupacabras, separated from his family for some reason, lost in the *pulga*.

CHAPTER TWENTY

The kids wandered for what felt like a long time. Lupita bought a bottle of water and they all shared it. Even Jersey seemed to have lost the scent, for when they let him poke his head out to pour some water on his tongue, he just looked around and took in the stalls, the sounds, and the smells, apparently delighted.

Suddenly, Mateo put out his hands. "Wait," he said. "I have an idea." He glanced at Jersey. "But, Elliot, you gotta make sure he stays hidden. The guy we're going to see would be very interested in your *amiguillo*."

Mateo led the others in a different direction. Soon, they were in an area where the corrugated roofs of the stalls cast long shadows. And yet, despite the shade, it wasn't any cooler here. The air was still and stifling. And it smelled of stale wood chips and . . . something else. Elliot tried to place the stench, but could not.

"What is this place?" Uchenna asked.

"It's kinda creepy," Elliot added.

Lupita said, "We don't come over here, usually. Mateo, where are you taking us?"

Mateo only said, "I told you. There's this guy . . ."

Then they saw him. A short, thin man with a broad cowboy hat and a smile like a rattlesnake's. And he was shaking hands with . . . a man who was dressed like a traditional English butler.

Uchenna grabbed Lupita, Elliot grabbed Mateo, and they held the siblings back.

"What are you doing?" Mateo said, but Uchenna shushed him.

They watched the butler pick up a large wooden crate and carry it away.

"Do you know that dude in the tuxedo?" Lupita asked in a whisper.

"That's Phipps," Uchenna replied quietly.

"Who's Phipps?"

"The Schmoke brothers' butler."

"I've heard of them . . . but where?" Lupita muttered. "Who are they again?"

"Tell you later," said Uchenna.

And Mateo said, "Yeah, come on. Let me introduce you to Charles."

Charles was the skinny man with the big hat and the rattlesnake smile. He was a vendor, and his "wares" were in dozens of glass cases: all the creatures that you would never want to encounter in the desert. Scorpions, black and brown, huge and tiny. A diamondback rattlesnake. A black widow, motionless, perched on a glass wall of a case. Elliot shuddered.

And then he saw the source of the strange smell that saturated this part of the *pulga*. A pile of dead mice sat on a table, their odor wafting out into the flea market. A sign next to the mice read, DINNER! 50¢ EACH!

Elliot turned to the vendor. Charles's boots looked like they were made from the skin of a snake, his belt buckle was large enough to serve a Thanksgiving turkey on, and from his wide-brimmed hat hung the hairless, wormlike tail of an opossum.

Mateo said to him, "Hi, Charles."

"Howdy, kid." Charles smiled. "Here to look at some more snakes?"

"Have you *bought snakes* from him?" Lupita demanded.

Mateo shook his head. "I just come here to look sometimes."

"But one day you're gonna buy," Charles said. "I can feel it. Gonna be one of my best customers one day."

"Maybe," Mateo said. "Right now, though, I have a question. We lost our, uh, our dog."

Uchenna and Elliot were staring at Charles. He'd just done business with Phipps. What *were* the Schmokes up to?

"I'm sorry to hear that," Charles replied.

"He's, uh, kind of an *ugly* dog," Mateo went on.

"We got a lot of ugly dogs down here," Charles said. "Champion ugly dogs, in fact."

"Yeah," said Mateo. "But this one had *spines*. Yellow spines. And very sharp teeth."

Suddenly, Charles's eyes got very, very thin, and the corners of his mouth took a sharp turn downward. "You don't say," Charles murmured.

"Have you seen him?" Mateo asked.

Charles looked down at the boy. After a moment, keeping his face very still, he said, "I can't say I have."

Uchenna leaned in. "You can't *say* that you have, or you *haven't*?"

Charles just looked at her.

"And," Uchenna added, "what did you sell to Phipps just now?"

"Who?"

"The butler."

"Oh." Charles held Uchenna in his gaze a long moment. A scorpion skittered across the glass of a case. "Now, look," Charles began, "my clients expect a degree of discretion. You buy a black widow, maybe you drop it in your mother-in-law's glove box—accidentally, of course—you don't want me blabbing about it here in the *pulga*, do ya?"

Uchenna put a hand on her hip. "You help people murder their *mothers*?"

"Mothers-*in-law*. It's a whole different thing. B'sides, who said anything about murder? It was an accident that he left that spider in that glove box."

Elliot suddenly felt a little sick. But Uchenna pressed on. "Did you find our dog?"

Charles looked at her. He didn't say a word.

"And did you sell it to Phipps?" Uchenna asked.

Charles kept looking.

Suddenly, Lupita was shouting at him. "You had no right to sell that . . . that *dog*! How dare you?! You just find someone's . . . someone's *dog* . . . and you sell it to the first person who asks?"

"This is a free country," Charles said. He spit through his teeth onto the ground. "The land of free enterprise. I am allowed to sell what I want to sell, to whom*ever* I want to sell it to."

"Not if it's not yours!" Lupita cried.

"And you're saying that weird puppy was yours? He didn't have any tags. No collar. And let's cut the bull"—he stuck a short finger in Lupita's face—"that was no *dog*. Now get lost."

CHAPTER TWENTY-ONE

The children stared at Charles. He had all ten of his fingers around his belt buckle and was staring right back.

And then Elliot stepped forward. He held up his hands. "I think there's been a misunderstanding."

Charles didn't reply. He just watched Elliot and waited.

"I think we all got off on the wrong foot," Elliot said. "You found a weird dog." He paused.

"Maybe I did, maybe I didn't," Charles answered.

"And you sold him," Elliot went on. "Sounds fine to me. It's a free country."

"That's what *I* said," Charles agreed.

"Right. A man can sell what he wants to whomever he wants."

"Exactly!" Charles said. "You and me, we see eye to eye."

Elliot nodded. "Now, there was a man wearing a crazy butler suit, who just left here with a big crate. His name is Phipps, and he works for the Schmoke brothers. You didn't happen to sell that dog to him, did you?"

Charles sucked on his teeth. "I told you, my clients expect privacy." But Charles seemed to be wrestling with something. Then he said, "You say he works for the Schmokes?"

It was Elliot's turn to get coy. He gazed stoically up at the vendor. The other kids shifted from foot to foot. "Maybe I did."

"Well," said Charles, "I hate them boys. Building that dumb wall."

Elliot and Uchenna looked at each other, eyes wide. "Ohhh . . ." said Uchenna. "That's what they're doing down there."

Charles jerked his finger at his glass cases. "More like trying to cut a man's business in half. I go collecting on both sides. And my clients live on both sides of the Río Grande, too. Takes me an hour to get through the checkpoint, and they always want to search my stuff. Walls ain't good for free enterprise." He paused. "Besides, I mighta found a lady friend in Nuevo Laredo. She's into poisonous frogs. You don't meet a woman like that every day. But she can't come over here so easy anymore. And that makes a feller lonely . . ."

"So you did sell it to Phipps, then?" Elliot asked.

Charles was jerked out of his reverie. "Huh? Oh." He spit again. "I suppose I did." And then he said, "Sorry."

A few minutes later, the kids were walking away from Charles's stall. Uchenna had just called Professor Fauna. As she put the phone back in her pocket, she said, "Okay. We're gonna meet them at the south entrance of the *pulga*."

"And then what?" asked Mateo.

Uchenna said, "We're going to the campus of Laredo College."

"Why?" asked Elliot.

"We have a date with the Schmoke brothers."

CHAPTER TWENTY-TWO

I t was getting late in the afternoon. The Cervantes family and the Unicorn Rescue Society team were in the minivan, nearing the edge of the college campus. To their left, they could see a shady, wooded area, separating the road from the wide and lazy Río Grande. All along the side of the road, a wrought-iron fence glittered in the sunlight.

Elliot tapped on the glass, pointing. "So this is the older fence. When did they build it?"

Dr. Cervantes sighed. "About a decade ago.

The college decided it didn't want people crossing the river onto its property. They put up the fence to discourage them. Waste of tax dollars. Completely useless in addressing the root issues. And if you don't solve the root issues, you're not going to solve the problem—folks will come in another way. Smuggled in trucks, across the Gulf of Mexico, or they'll get here the way *most* undocumented immigrants do—fly legally into the US and then simply overstay their visas. But they wanted this fence because they're scared of people coming over from the other side—Ooh! Our neighbors who happen to live on the other side of the border! How scary!" Dr. Cervantes scoffed. "Several of us professors tried to talk sense into the college leadership, but they called us out-of-touch, snobby elitists. They build a useless fence out of fancy wrought iron, and *we're* the out-of-touch ones? Outrageous!"

"Well, to be fair," Mr. Cervantes pointed out, "you did call the president and the trustees a 'gaggle of gaseous geese.'"

"True. Kind of undercut my argument, didn't it?" she said, winking.

Mateo pointed. "And there's the wall."

Uchenna and Elliot pressed their faces against the window of the minivan.

The wrought-iron fence continued into a construction area, where it ended, and a tall, solid concrete wall stood in its place. The concrete wall extended a hundred yards or so, and then the wrought-iron fence started again, passing out of the construction area.

"That's weird," said Elliot. "Are they doing it in small batches or something?"

Israel Cervantes shook his head.

"No. A judge stopped

construction a few weeks back, but the Schmokes appealed. We'll hear the new decision today." Backhoes and diggers and bulldozers were idling near the wall inside the construction site, puffing black smoke into the bright blue air. "These construction folks seem mighty sure of winning that appeal."

His wife gripped the steering wheel more tightly. "Believe me, the Schmoke brothers have many influential government friends in their ample pockets."

Professor Fauna growled deep in his throat. Jersey, sitting at Uchenna's feet, imitated the sound.

"Look!" Elliot gasped. "It's Phipps!"

There was a gate at the entrance to the construction site. A security guard punched a button, and the gate slid back to let a stiffly formal man in a butler's uniform walk through.

In his white-gloved hands was a wooden crate.

"Choopi!" Mateo exclaimed. *"Mamá, ¡estaciónate!* Doesn't matter where. Just pull over!"

Dr. Cervantes slowed the minivan but kept driving. *"Espérate, m'ijo,"* she said. "We need to think this through. We can't just rush into that place. The guard would stop us."

Uchenna, leaning over Mateo for a better look, said, "Phipps is going into that office trailer!"

The butler climbed three steps into a shiny mobile office. Just as he opened the door, a horrible whine split the air. It wasn't the high whistle that the chupacabras had used to put Jersey to sleep, but a high-pitched whistle that made your skin crawl. Jersey snarled.

"*What* is that *sound?*" Dr. Cervantes asked.

"Oh!" said Elliot, getting excited. "It sounds like *another* type of chupacabras whistle! This will be the third I've documented—well, *will* document. The first was the low, hypnotic whistle. The second was a higher, shrill whine—like Choopi was complaining or upset. This whistle sounds almost like a scream! Speaking of documentation— Professor, when were you going to tell me about the *Proceedings of the Unicorn Rescue Society?*"

"What, Elliot? I don't know! Not now!" replied Professor Fauna. "Oh, that whistle is unbearable!"

Indeed, inside the minivan, everyone was covering their ears, and Phipps was grimacing as he tried to get the shrieking crate into the office trailer.

"He's so upset!" Lupita cried. "We've got to help him!"

"But how are we going to get in there?" Professor Fauna said.

"You know what?" Dr. Cervantes replied. "I was wrong." She steered the minivan right up to  the guard station. Everyone else in the van suddenly went pale. What was Dr. Cervantes doing? She leaned her head out the window.

A young man with a construction hat walked up to the side of the van. "Dr. Cervantes!" he said. *"¿Qué anda haciendo por acá?"*

Dr. Cervantes frowned. "Is that any way to talk to your favorite professor? No *'buenas tardes'*? No 'How can I help you today, Dr. Cervantes?'"

The young man blushed. "Sorry, Dr. Cervantes. How can I help you?"

"I'm here on university business," she said. "Gotta park in there and talk to some of the big *hombres*. How's your mother?"

The young man smiled. *"Está muy bien. Gracias.* I'm not really supposed to let you in without an appointment or something, but . . ."

Dr. Cervantes flashed him her widest smile.

"But you *are* my favorite professor, so . . ." The young man stepped back and waved her through.

Dr. Cervantes waved at him and drove into the construction site.

"Wow," said her husband. "You must have given him a really good grade."

Dr. Cervantes chuckled. "Are you kidding? He got a C-minus."

"Seriously?" Mateo exclaimed. "And he still likes you?"

"Yes, he likes me, *m'ijo. And* he respects me. Which is even more important."

Dr. Cervantes steered the minivan past the guard station and over the dirt and gravel ground of the construction site.

They were inside.

CHAPTER TWENTY-THREE

D r. Cervantes drove the van around to the back of the construction site, out of view of the Schmokes' office trailer, and parked next to the wrought-iron border fence.

Everyone piled out of the minivan. The children all found themselves peering through the bars, across the chaparral, to the Río Grande, and into Mexico beyond. The terrain there was exactly the same as the terrain here in Texas. In fact, the buildings looked the same, too. There was a big sign, in the distance, in Spanish. But there were signs in Spanish on the US side as well. Except for the river and the fence, you would have no idea where Mexico ended and the United States began.

Lupita suddenly said, "Did you hear that?" She was looking through the fence, past the wooded riverbank, down to the slow-moving waters of the Río Grande.

"Choopi?" Uchenna asked. "I think I can still hear him whistling . . ."

"No, not him." Lupita's eyes went wide, and she took a step back as she lifted her arm and pointed. "Them!"

From the other side of the border fence came a cacophony of whistling. Dr. Cervantes, Mr. Cervantes, Professor Fauna, Elliot, Uchenna, Lupita, and Mateo all looked around wildly. Elliot peeked inside the backpack, to see if Jersey had gone rigid again. He had not. Instead, he was shivering. The whistling grew louder. This was not the hypnotic whistle, or the shriek. It was more like the whining noise, but it was longer and sadder. Like a dog howling at the moon.

"Look!" Professor Fauna cried. "There they are!"

Elliot turned to look—which was when Jersey burst out of the backpack that Elliot had neglected to close and began to dive toward a gap in the border fence.

Uchenna leaped after him, catching the little Jersey Devil just before he wriggled between the iron bars. She pulled him tight against her chest.

"Whew," she muttered. "That was close. Elliot, you need to . . ."

Her words trailed off as she looked up. The professor was still pointing. There, amid the trees on the near bank of the Río Grande, stood a dozen chupacabras—like Choopi, but bigger, eyes smaller relative to the terrifying faces. These were adults. Their eyes glowed golden, their hairless bodies dripped water as if they'd just swum

across the river, their quills were rigid and sharp. One of them bared its stiletto teeth. Choopi suddenly shrieked from inside the office trailer. The whole pack whistled mournfully to the skies.

"Oh, snap," muttered Mateo. "It's his pack, isn't it?"

The humans and chupacabras stared at one another through the bars.

"This is how he got separated," Lupita murmured. "The fence."

Dr. Cervantes was nodding. "He must have wandered off, wriggled through, and then couldn't figure out how to get back."

"They look so sad," said Uchenna.

"And he *sounds* so sad," Elliot said, listening to Choopi's cries.

"He sounds like my friend Andrés," Mateo mumbled. "Plus the weird whistling, of course."

"Enough of this moaning!" Professor Fauna announced. "Let us rescue this young chupacabras and reunite him with his family before we all drown in a new Río Grande of tears!" He raised a finger. "So—"

"*WAIT!*" Uchenna hissed. She pointed away from the border fence.

A limousine was pulling in through the guarded gate of the construction site. It parked near the trailer. The chauffeur got out and opened the back doors. Two balding men emerged, dressed in white suits and with rich blue shirts, one tall and thin, the other short and fat.

Milton and Edmund Schmoke.

The door of the trailer burst open, and Phipps came strutting down the stairs.

"Welcome, sirs!" he called with sycophantic delight. "You simply will not believe the gift I have obtained for you. The perfect addition to your growing collection of rarities."

"Excellent!" Edmund exclaimed, his green eyes crinkling at the thought. "Something good finally emerges from this horrid, backwoods inferno."

"Yes, about time we reaped a profit," Milton agreed. "What is this rare item, Phipps?"

Pausing for dramatic effect, the butler uttered a single word. "Chupacabras."

"*Really?* You don't say!" Edmund gushed. "How many?"

Phipps looked confused. "Just the one."

"Tsk-tsk! You said 'chupacabras'! How many?"

"I did, sir, but—" Phipps attempted to explain, but Milton cut him off.

"No excuses, Phipps! We demand precision!"

Phipps opened his mouth to explain once more and then decided against it.

"No matter," said Edmund. "Show us this little addition to our collection."

And the three of them climbed the steps into the office trailer.

"Well," Lupita growled, "how do we rescue Choopi now?"

Dr. Cervantes pulled her university ID from her back pocket. "Don't worry. I've got a plan."

CHAPTER TWENTY-FOUR

M ilton Schmoke's fingers were poised over the wooden crate on the desk. A plaintive whistling could be heard from inside.

"The famous chupacabra," Milton murmured.

"Chupacabras, sir," Phipps interjected. "You see, the word *chupacabra* means—"

Milton straightened up. "Phipps, you've just lost a week's pay for attempting to correct me. Keep talking. I *love* saving money on labor costs."

"Quite right," Edmund agreed.

Just then, a sharp rapping rang out from the door of the Schmoke brothers' trailer.

"Who could that be?" Edmund exclaimed.

Phipps pulled himself up, straightened his starched white shirt, tried to momentarily forget that he'd just lost a whole week's income, and opened the trailer door.

A tall woman, with long brown hair pulled back in a bun under a hard hat, was standing on the ground in front of the trailer's steps. She held up her university ID and announced, "I'm here as an inspector on behalf of the university. Are you in charge?"

Phipps sniffed. "I most certainly am *not*. But if you'd like to see who *is* in charge, you will need an appointment. And I'm afraid there are no appointments available." He began to close the door.

But Dr. Cervantes said, "We'll be towing the bulldozers within the hour then."

Inside the trailer, Edmund and Milton, who had been waiting to open the precious crate until the inspector went away, both let out an indignant "What?!"

"Let me speak to this impertinent woman!" Edmund bellowed, waddling over to the door and pushing Phipps out of the way.

"Tell her what's what!" Milton shouted.

Edmund, round and self-satisfied as a toad, stood over Dr. Cervantes, because of the height of the trailer. Otherwise, he would have been much shorter than she. He said, "I don't know what bureaucratic hole you crawled out of, but I suggest you crawl back into it. I am a job creator, not a parasitic civil servant. Also, my machines are operating legally."

"Apologies, *méndiga sanguijuela*," Dr. Cervantes said, "but you are on a government contract, using tax-payer dollars to build a wall on university land. We can discuss who's the parasite later. Right now, bring your *cara egoísta* out here before I get some very large tow trucks to impound your machines, this trailer, and you. *¿Captaste?*"

Edmund turned beet red. "What did you say to me? Just what exactly did you say? Say it again in English! This is America!"

Dr. Cervantes turned and walked away from the trailer. "People have been speaking Spanish on this land long before the Estados-Unidos even existed, *colonialista ignorante*," she said over her shoulder. "And before that, we spoke Coahuilteco here. But if you want me to use English to get your *traserote* off this land, I'd be happy to." Dr. Cervantes whipped out her phone, pretended to dial a number, and then, after a moment, said, "Fred, I'm gonna need a heavy-duty flatbed tow truck down at the community college—"

"Wait!" Edmund cried, waddling after her. "You can't do that!"

Milton, inside the trailer, leaped to his feet. "Stop that woman! Phipps, do something!"

Phipps hustled out the door right behind Milton, and they all began hurrying after Dr. Cervantes, who continued to stride away from them, telling "Fred" about all the machinery she'd need to tow the Schmokes' equipment away.

Uchenna, Elliot, Lupita, and Mateo, crouching just out of sight behind some orange barrels, chuckled. "Your mom is *good*," Uchenna said quietly.

"My mom has many talents," Lupita agreed, "but ticking off powerful people is definitely her greatest."

"The coast is clear," Mateo said, as the Schmokes and Phipps followed Dr. Cervantes around a giant digger. "Let's do this thing."

CHAPTER TWENTY-FIVE

Mateo led the way up the metal steps of the trailer and through the flimsy door. The other kids followed him.

The crate was sitting on the desk, and Choopi's plaintive whines echoed from inside.

Mateo and Lupita each took one side of Choopi's crate, Elliot opened the trailer door, and Uchenna led the way out.

The Schmokes and Phipps were nowhere to be seen, nor was Dr. Cervantes. When the kids carried the crate around the back of the trailer, Professor Fauna and Mr. Cervantes were waiting for them.

Mateo, Lupita, Elliot, and Uchenna all turned and gave one another daps and high fives. Jersey poked his head out of his backpack and started to growl at the crate.

"Uh, guys—" said Lupita.

But Elliot quickly unwrapped an almond bar, tossed it into the pack, and when Jersey dove down after it, he zipped up the backpack.

They had agreed to wait for Dr. Cervantes to return before they released Choopi. But now that his crate was so near the fence, his family's whining whistles had become unbearable. Choopi scratched and shrieked from inside the crate.

"We gotta let him out," Uchenna announced. "This is torture!"

"I agree!" said Elliot.

"My mom is gonna be heartbroken that she can't see this reunion," Mateo said. "She's studied these guys for years. This is once in a lifetime!"

Lupita said, "She'll be back any minute, I know it."

Choopi scratched and whined and whimpered. The adult chupacabras, with their golden eyes that flashed red in the sunlight, whistled and paced anxiously.

Mr. Cervantes set his chin. "I'll go find her. Wait five minutes. The chupacabras have been waiting for a lot longer than that. If I'm not back in five, let Choopi go. *¿Entendieron, chamacos?*"

"*Sí*, Daddy." Lupita nodded. "We'll do it."

"Be careful," Mateo added.

Mr. Cervantes kissed them each on the forehead, flashed a thumbs-up to Elliot, Uchenna, and Professor Fauna, and hurried around the office trailer to look for his wife.

One, two, and three minutes passed. He did not come back.

Four minutes passed, and he did not come back.

Five minutes passed, and he did not come back.

They looked at one another nervously.

Six minutes.

Seven minutes.

Choopi's whistles were becoming groans.

"This is awful," Uchenna groaned.

"What do you think is going on over there?" Lupita asked, biting her thumbnail.

Mateo wiped sweat from his brow. "Let's let Choopi go."

Professor Fauna was nervously chewing at

the side of a calloused finger. Then he stopped. "Wait. I shall find them!" he announced.

"NO!" said Uchenna and Elliot at the same time.

"The Schmokes will recognize you!" Uchenna exclaimed.

"*¿Y luego, qué?* We have Choopi. If you see me coming back trussed like a turkey, you let him go, *pronto.* Yes?"

"And what if *you* don't come back?"

"Then you let him go. And call the police. Uchenna, you have your phone, yes?"

Uchenna nodded. All the children looked upset. The chupacabras on the other side of the fence were whistle-howling again.

"*Defende Fabulosa,*" Professor Fauna said quietly.

And they all replied, "*Protege Mythica.*"

CHAPTER TWENTY-SIX

One minute went by.

Two minutes.

"Goodness gracious," Elliot muttered.

Three minutes.

Four minutes.

"Goodness gracious, goodness gracious," Elliot said again, holding his arms and rocking back and forth. The chupacabras whistled.

Five minutes.

Six minutes. The pack of chupacabras kept

creeping forward, more and more agitated, quills rigid, teeth bared.

"Goodness gracious, goodness gracious, goodness gr—"

"Let's do it," Uchenna interrupted. "Let's release Choopi and call the police."

Mateo and Lupita looked at each other, and then at Uchenna. They nodded. "Okay. Let's—"

"*¡Hijos!*" Alejandra Cervantes appeared around the corner of the mobile trailer.

"*¡Mamá!*" Mateo cried.

Mr. Cervantes appeared right behind her. "Dad!" Lupita shouted.

They both ran to their parents and gave them tight hugs.

"It's okay," Mr. Cervantes was saying. "Your mamá had it all under control the whole time."

"Of course I did," said Dr. Cervantes, stroking her son's head as he hugged her. "I just needed to take the Schmokes on a very long tour of their worksite, complete with eighteen violations for

mis-parked bulldozers, cranes that were painted the wrong color, and a very ugly choice of concrete for the wall."

"And where's Professor Fauna?" Uchenna asked.

Dr. and Mr. Cervantes both released their children.

"What do you mean?" Mr. Cervantes asked. "He didn't stay with you?" He saw the unopened crate. "And you didn't release Choopi?"

The kids shook their heads. *"Ay, caray,"* Dr. Cervantes said. "I imagine the Schmokes are headed back here now. They might have already spotted Erasmo. Which would be very bad."

"Let's release Choopi now!" said Elliot. "We can't afford to wait any—"

"¡Amigos míos!"

Everyone spun around.

"Look who I have found!" It was Professor Fauna. With someone that nobody had expected to see.

Bob Braunfels, the rancher.

CHAPTER TWENTY-SEVEN

Bob Braunfels gave a little wave as he approached the group. In his other hand he carried a homemade sign.

"What is going on?" Dr. Cervantes demanded.

"Everyone is coming here!" Professor Fauna replied. "To the construction site!"

"Everyone?" said Mr. Cervantes. "Who is everyone?"

"From city hall," said Professor Fauna. "The

judge has announced his verdict. He has extended the stay another three weeks."

The Cervantes family threw up their hands in disgust.

"That's it? Three weeks? And then what?" Mateo fumed.

Professor Fauna shrugged. "No one knows. They claim they need more time to study it."

Lupita snorted.

"Indeed. *Everyone* is angry. And they are all marching onto campus," Professor Fauna went on. "Which is how I ran into my friend here."

Dr. Cervantes objected. "Bob Braunfels is your *friend*? He wants that wall built more than the Schmokes want to build it!"

"Howdy, Alejandra," Mr. Braunfels said, speaking for the first time and tipping his hat to Dr. Cervantes.

And then, from behind him, appeared a boy about Mateo's age. He had straight black hair that was swept across his forehead and a serious look in his eyes. He was also carrying a home-made sign.

"*Hola,* Mateo," he said. "Hi, Lupita."

Mateo exclaimed, "Andrés! *¿Qué haces aquí?*"

"And what are you doing with *him*?" Lupita said, pointing at Bob Braunfels.

"What d'ya mean, what's he doing with me?" Mr. Braunfels said, putting a hand on the boy's shoulder. "Andrés *lives* with me."

Mateo turned to the group. "This is my friend that I was telling you about. Whose parents are in detention some-where." He turned to Andrés. "But I thought you were living with our prin-cipal, Mrs. Braunfels?" Then Mateo's mouth fell open and his eyes got really wide. "Oh . . . ," he said.

"That'd be my wife," the rancher said with a chuckle. Then he picked up his sign. It read, NO WALL, NO LAW in big black letters.

Mr. Braunfels went on. "We came for the protest, but the professor here said he had something he wanted to show us. Is that right, Professor?"

Mateo said, "Wait—Andrés, you're helping Mr. Braunfels protest in *favor* of the wall?"

"What?" said Andrés. *"¿Estás loco?"* He spun his sign around. In bright blue capitals it read, SOMOS UNA FAMILIA—WE ARE ONE FAMILY (AND WHERE IS MINE?)

Everyone paused for a moment as they read the sign. A lump formed in Elliot's throat, and tears collected in the corners of Uchenna's eyes.

"Andrés and I don't agree on much," Mr. Braunfels said. "But we both believe in free speech. And," he added, suddenly very serious, "I *don't* think kids should be separated from their parents. Not ever."

"I am glad you have mentioned this!" Professor Fauna exclaimed. "That is why you are here. Elliot, Uchenna, you have not released it yet?"

They shook their heads.

"Then show Mr. Braunfels what is in the box!"

Elliot and Uchenna hesitated. The crate sat behind them on the ground. A plaintive whistle was echoing from within.

Dr. Cervantes stepped between Mr. Braunfels and the crate. "Erasmo, why on earth do you think you can trust this man?"

Professor Fauna drew himself up to his full height. "Because those we disagree with are not always our enemies, Alejandra. Now, *por favor*, show him."

CHAPTER TWENTY-EIGHT

Mr. Braunfels and Andrés hovered over the box, staring down at the small chupacabras huddled in the shadows of one corner.

"Poor little guy looks scared," said Mr. Braunfels.

"No," said Andrés. "He looks sad. Trust me. I can tell."

Uchenna said, "We call him Choopi."

"Choopi," the rancher repeated. "I like that name."

Andrés said, "I'd call him 'Bloodguzzler.'"

Mr. Braunfels laughed and said to the others, "Told you we don't agree on much."

Suddenly, Choopi straightened up and whistled. On the other side of the fence, a dozen whistles answered him.

Mr. Braunfels and Andrés looked up, their eyes wide. Dr. Cervantes said, "His family."

"Well, what are we waiting for?" Andrés said. "Let's reunite them!"

Mr. Cervantes said, "I agree. Let's go. Bob, will you help me out here?"

Mr. Cervantes, the Mexican American *curandero*, and Mr. Braunfels, the Anglo rancher, put their hands on the young chupacabras and hoisted him, wriggling and whistling, out of the crate.

The family of chupacabras had been crouching in the shade of the mesquite trees or hiding behind rocks, calling for their pup. But when they saw the humans lift Choopi out of the crate, they stood up and trotted into the sunlight.

Mr. Braunfels almost dropped the box. "Heck," he said. "That's a lot of them."

Indeed, there were about a dozen.

"Those golden eyes and yellow spines make them look really scary," Elliot said. "But that's just because people don't know much about them."

Uchenna added, "People are always afraid of what they don't know much about."

"And they drink blood," Andrés added.

"So do mosquitoes," Lupita retorted.

One member of the chupacabras family trotted all the way up to the fence.

"Do you think—" Elliot began.

"*Su madre*," Andrés said.

Mateo translated, "His mother."

Choopi's whines became desperate, and he began scrabbling at the men's arms, trying to escape.

Lupita started to count, and all the kids immediately joined in: "*¡Uno*, two, *tres!*"

Mr. Braunfels and Mr. Cervantes released Choopi. He sprang out of their arms and leaped at the fence.

His mother, on the other side, reared up on her hind legs and scratched at the wrought iron with her forepaws. Choopi threw himself against the fence once, and then again.

"Come on, little guy!" Dr. Cervantes said. Then Choopi found the spaces between the bars. He was just small enough to wriggle through. *"There you go,"* Dr. Cervantes whispered.

The mother chupacabras and her child danced around each other, leaping and yipping and whistling high, piercing whistles.

"That must be their happy whistle," murmured Elliot. "I'll write that down. Later."

They watched the ecstatic reunion of the chupacabras family. The others had come out of the shade now, and Choopi was running from one to another, tackling them, rolling in the dust with them, and then jumping up and sprinting off to another one.

Mr. Braunfels sniffed heavily and dragged his arm across his eyes.

Andrés wasn't even trying to hide his tears. They were running steadily and silently down his cheeks.

Mr. Cervantes put his arm around Dr. Cervantes's shoulders.

Lupita put her arm around Mateo's shoulders. He didn't even shrug it off.

And then, behind them, they heard something that made the hair stand up on every human's neck.

Whistling.

They spun around.

CHAPTER TWENTY-NINE

Emerging from the holes that had been dug in the earth of the hill facing the Río Grande were a half-dozen chupacabras. On the American side of the wall.

"What the—" Mr. Braunfels said.

"Did they *all* get across?" Mr. Cervantes said.

These new chupacabras were staring at the humans. One began to growl. Its yellow spines stood up on its back.

"Uh-oh," said Elliot. "That one doesn't look happy."

Suddenly, the spines on the backs of all the chupacabras on the American side stood up, and the growls became shrill whistles. Shrill, angry whistles. The chupacabras started down the slope, toward the humans.

"*¿Qué pasa?* Are they going to hurt us?" Andrés asked.

"*No creo, pero* . . . it kinda looks like it," Mateo answered, backing away. But then he stopped. His back had hit the iron fence.

"Nowhere to go," said Lupita.

Indeed, the chupacabras on the flanks were hemming the group of humans in.

"I thought they didn't hurt people?" Mr. Cervantes asked.

"There is so much we don't know about these creatures," Dr. Cervantes replied.

"I, for one, thought that they did not hurt people," Professor Fauna added. "Should we run? Maybe we should run . . ."

But Bob Braunfels, in a very soft voice, said,

"Hold on." And then he pursed his lips and started whistling, quiet and low. The chupacabras all looked at him.

He kept whistling. Then he said, "Ain't nothing to worry about, doggies. We're friendly here." And he whistled some more.

"He knows chupacabras whistles?!" Elliot hissed. *"How?"*

Andrés whispered back, *"What are you talking about? That's how he talks to all the animals on the ranch."*

Mr. Braunfels had his hands up, and was whistling sweetly and softly. The chupacabras were still coming toward the people, but they appeared less agitated.

Uchenna glanced over her shoulder. The chupacabras on the other side of the fence had calmed down, too.

"Okay, folks," said Mr. Braunfels, "let's just step to the side." Following his lead, everyone sidestepped away from the chupacabras. Mr. Braunfels stopped whistling.

And the chupacabras charged.

But they didn't charge the humans. They charged the fence.

The six American chupacabras ran down to the barrier, and the chupacabras on the Mexican side began jumping and running. The ones on the American side jumped and ran with them.

Everyone stared. Most of them felt very confused.

"Do we need to help them get back, too?" Lupita asked.

"I guess . . . ?" Elliot replied.

But Professor Fauna was shaking his head. "No, *amigos*. You do not understand."

The chupacabras on both sides yapped and whistled and jumped and spun. It looked like they were dancing. Like a big family reunion. A big family reunion, with a wrought-iron fence running down the middle.

Dr. Cervantes wiped a tear from her cheek. "Don't you see? We were all wrong. The chupacabras don't live in Mexico and come across the border. Nor do they live in the United States. They live on *both* sides. They always have." She sighed. "Governments create borders. But for families—of chupacabras and people—borders just keep them apart."

The humans stood in silence, watching the chupacabras leap and play and whistle at one another, on both sides of the fence.

"*¿Qué vamos a hacer?*" Andrés murmured. "What are we gonna do?"

"About what?" asked Dr. Cervantes.

"About this." He gestured at the chupacabras, their family reunion divided by iron. "We can't just let them stay this way."

"*Amigo mío*," Professor Fauna said with a deep sigh, "this is a problem that the community of Laredo will have to solve."

"The whole *country* is gonna have to solve it," Mr. Braunfels added. He sighed heavily, too. "You know I believe in strong borders. But I gotta go with Andrés here. This isn't right."

"Why don't we all go back to our house?" suggested Mr. Cervantes. "And see if we can't start the process of figuring it out."

Professor Fauna held up his hands. "Wait. I have one crucial question."

Dr. Cervantes said, "Yes, Erasmo, *tenemos más guacamole*."

The professor looked shocked. "How did you know I would ask about the guacamole?"

Everyone laughed.

CHAPTER THIRTY

Mr. Braunfels and Andrés followed the champagne minivan back to the Cervanteses' house for some *aguas frescas* and fresh guacamole. Professor Fauna was very grateful.

"Rescuing mythical creatures works up an appetite," he managed to say around mouthfuls of it.

The five kids had huddled around Uchenna's phone, watching a livestream of the protest.

"So, what's the news?" Bob asked, setting down his glass.

"Looks like the Schmokes got fed up," Uchenna said.

"Yeah," added Mateo. "They're heading back to New Jersey. They released a statement that they're passing on the job. Something about onerous rules and regulations about the colors of cranes?"

Everyone laughed, Dr. Cervantes the loudest of all.

Elliot stretched. "Speaking of going back to New Jersey . . . ," he said.

Wiping green splotches from his beard, the professor nodded and stood. "*Amigos míos,* our time together has come to an end. But while we have reunited Choopi with his family, the work of the Unicorn Rescue Society is not done. We saw those chupacabras, separated by that wall. Until they are free to roam their natural habitats, their species is in danger."

"As are all the cows around here," Mr. Braunfels added.

"And so," Professor Fauna went on, turning

to Dr. Cervantes, "Alejandra. Surely, you see the value in our work now. Will you reconsider your decision? Will you join us again and seek a long-term solution for these chupacabras?"

She shook her head and stood up, looking him directly in the eyes, her expression severe. "You have a lot of nerve asking me that—" she began.

Mateo and Lupita took sharp breaths. Uchenna's eyes went wide. Elliot thought about sticking his fingers in his ears in case she used adult language.

"Without asking my family to join as well," Dr. Cervantes concluded, her eyes glittering.

It took Fauna a second to understand, then he laughed. "Oh, dearest Alejandra, of course!"

Bob Braunfels cleared his throat. "Erasmo, the Cervantes family ain't gonna be able to do this alone. They're gonna need assistance. From the whole community. On *every* side. Besides, I want to help." He stood up. "I reckon you're gonna need to induct me, too."

"*¡Y a mí también!*" said Andrés. "Me too."

For a moment, Uchenna thought the professor might start to cry. But he stood straighter, taller, and addressed the friends before him. He demanded of them all, "Do you swear to defend the imaginary and protect the mythical?"

"Yes!" they cried as one.

"*Defende Fabulosa!*" the professor intoned.

And the Cervantes family replied, "*Protege*

Mythica!" Then they taught Mr. Braunfels and Andrés how to say it, too.

"*¡Pues, bienvenidos, amigos míos!*" Professor Fauna announced. "Welcome to the Unicorn Rescue Society!"

Soon everyone was hugging, and Elliot edged closer to the professor to ask the question that had been bugging him for hours.

"Uh, Professor . . . Can I be the editor of the *Proceedings*?"

Erasmo Fauna looked down at him with a wistful smile. "Ah, dear friend, I am afraid that publication is quite defunct."

Elliot's shoulders slumped in disappointment.

"But perhaps you and I can revive it. Yes. I believe I would like that very much."

CHAPTER THIRTY-ONE

The group spilled out into the driveway, where the *Phoenix* sat wingless and not particularly ready for the return journey.

"Keep the chupacabras safe," the professor instructed, as he shook their hands one by one. "And be on the lookout for other creatures."

"We're going on vacation to Monterrey this summer," Dr. Cervantes said, drawing Professor Fauna into an unexpected hug. "I'll check on the *gente pájaro* for you, Erasmo."

For a moment the professor held her more tightly, then he stepped toward the plane, calling over his shoulder.

"Elliot, Uchenna. Let us go. Your families will be unhappy if we are late."

The sun was already sinking in the sky, just like Elliot's heart. *Impossible. We won't make it. My mom will kill me.*

Mateo bumped his fists against Elliot's. "So, we're down for a FaceGram this weekend, yeah?"

"A what?" Elliot rubbed his knuckles, confused.

Uchenna finished hugging Lupita and laughed. "Don't worry. I'll explain it to him on the way home. Andrés, you're part of the URS family now. We need updates. Weekly."

Andrés smiled broadly, his eyes glistening. Elliot and Uchenna clambered into the plane and waved good-bye to their friends one last time as the professor backed the plane out of the driveway and into the street.

"*Y allá vamos*," the professor muttered, fiddling with the radio knobs. "Back in time for dinner. I think I shall make guacamole."

"There's no way we're getting home in time for dinner!" Elliot objected. "It's a thirty-hour drive!"

"Time zones, *mi amigo*, time zones," the professor assured him as they drove off. "They work wonders."

"No they don't!" Elliot insisted.

"They have on all our past adventures," Uchenna pointed out with a shrug.

Elliot sighed.

"*Pues, nada.* Off into the sunset!" shouted Erasmo Fauna as the sound of mariachis filled the cabin.

"But this is the wrong direction!" cried Elliot.

No one was listening. Uchenna and the professor were loudly singing along to an upbeat mariachi tune.

And Jersey?

He kept staring out the window, his tongue flicking in and out.

A squeaky sound emerged. Elliot leaned in close, and he couldn't help but smile.

The little guy was trying to whistle.

A HISTORY OF

The Secret Order of the Unicorn

(Being the History of the Secret Organization, Founded in the Year 789, That Exists to Protect Unicorns from All Humans Who Might Hurt Them)

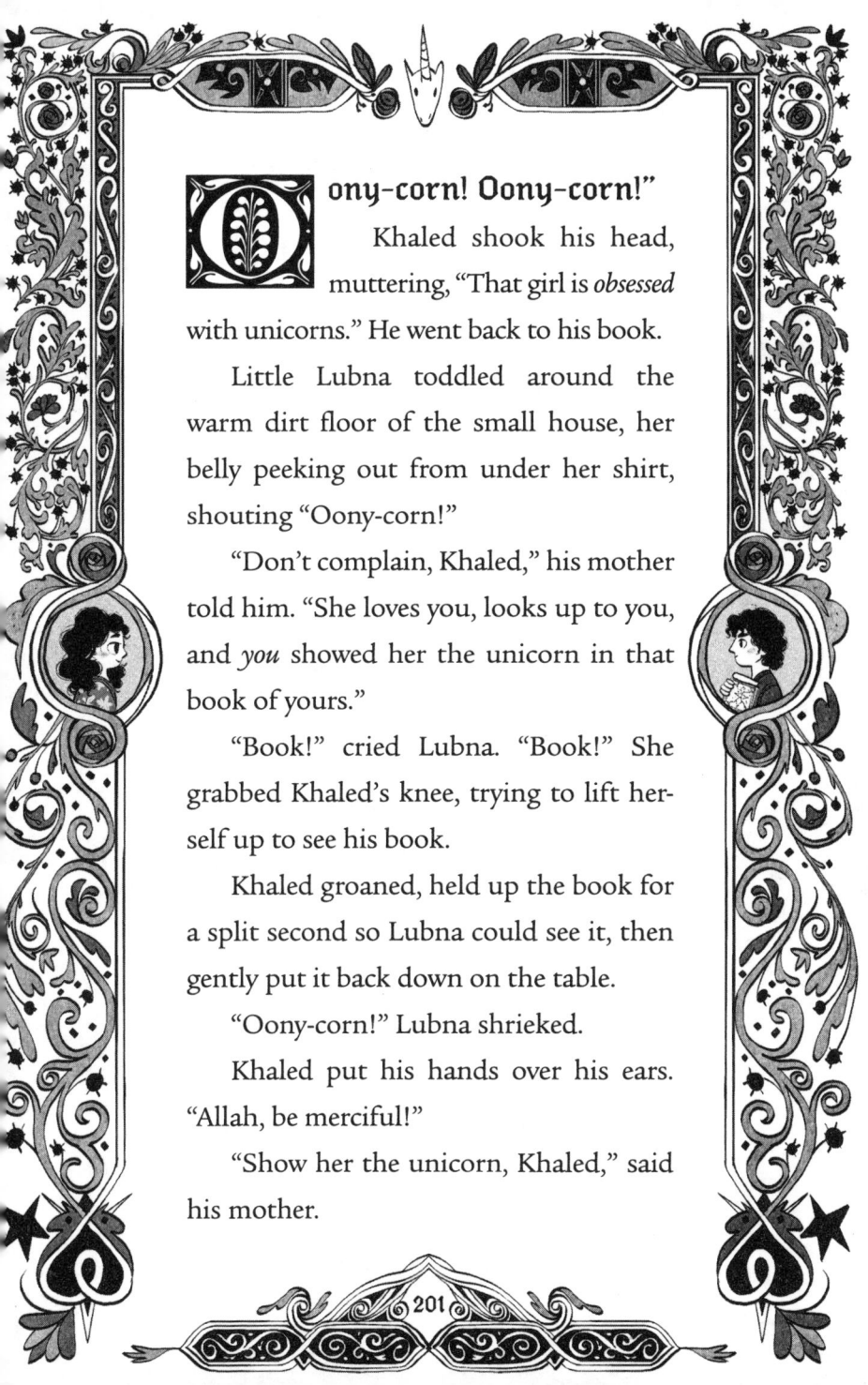

"ony-corn! Oony-corn!"

Khaled shook his head, muttering, "That girl is *obsessed* with unicorns." He went back to his book.

Little Lubna toddled around the warm dirt floor of the small house, her belly peeking out from under her shirt, shouting "Oony-corn!"

"Don't complain, Khaled," his mother told him. "She loves you, looks up to you, and *you* showed her the unicorn in that book of yours."

"Book!" cried Lubna. "Book!" She grabbed Khaled's knee, trying to lift herself up to see his book.

Khaled groaned, held up the book for a split second so Lubna could see it, then gently put it back down on the table.

"Oony-corn!" Lubna shrieked.

Khaled put his hands over his ears. "Allah, be merciful!"

"Show her the unicorn, Khaled," said his mother.

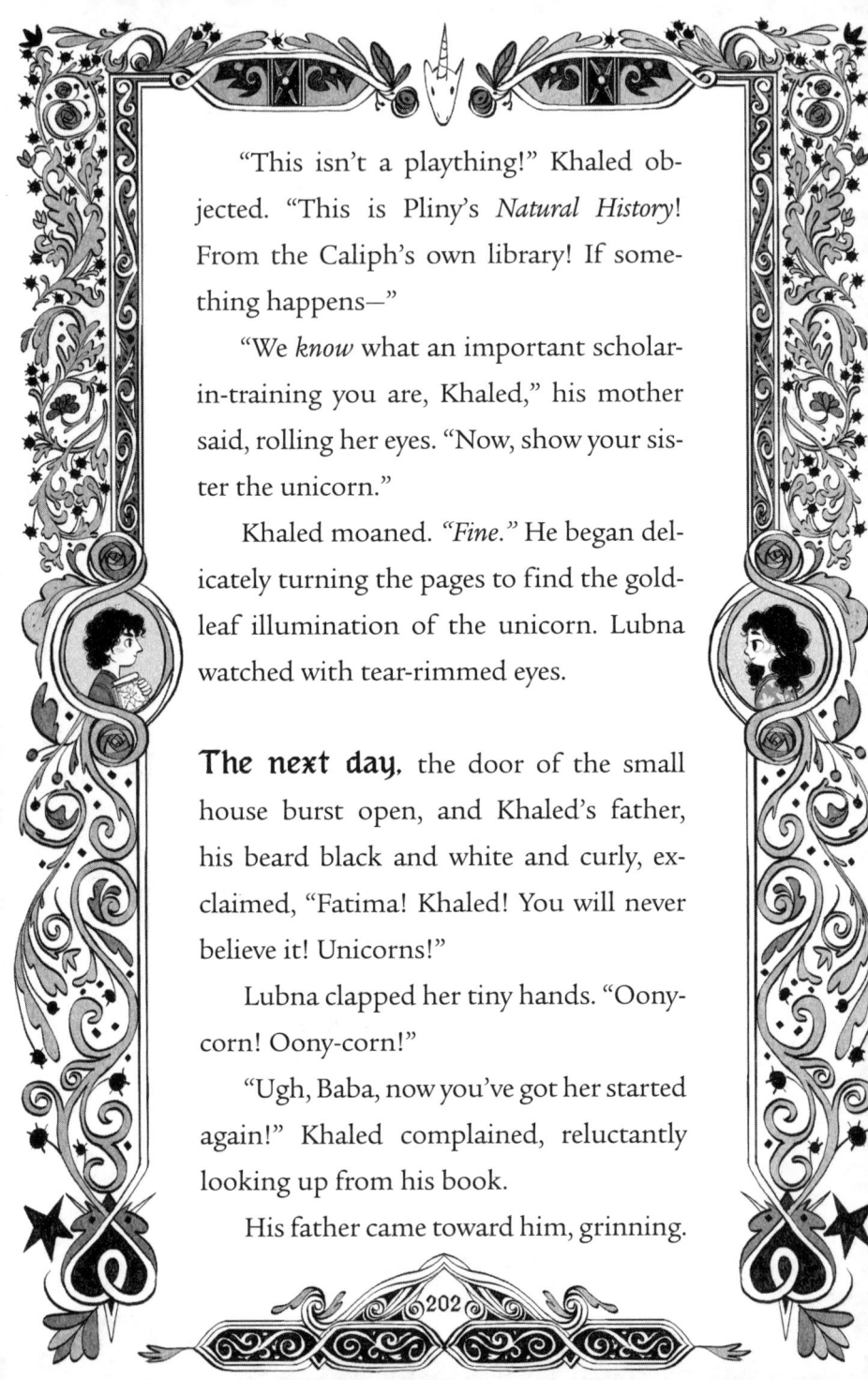

"This isn't a plaything!" Khaled objected. "This is Pliny's *Natural History*! From the Caliph's own library! If something happens—"

"We *know* what an important scholar-in-training you are, Khaled," his mother said, rolling her eyes. "Now, show your sister the unicorn."

Khaled moaned. *"Fine."* He began delicately turning the pages to find the gold-leaf illumination of the unicorn. Lubna watched with tear-rimmed eyes.

The next day, the door of the small house burst open, and Khaled's father, his beard black and white and curly, exclaimed, "Fatima! Khaled! You will never believe it! Unicorns!"

Lubna clapped her tiny hands. "Oony-corn! Oony-corn!"

"Ugh, Baba, now you've got her started again!" Khaled complained, reluctantly looking up from his book.

His father came toward him, grinning.

He grabbed Khaled by the shoulders. "You think *that* got her started? Wait till you hear *this*. There is a whole *herd* of unicorns coming toward town *right now*."

"*Oony-corn!!!*" Lubna shouted, spinning in circles.

"Baba, unicorns aren't *real*. Pliny was describing the rhinoceros. He'd just never seen one, so he described it wrong."

"Khaled, I think you should come and see for yourself." His father was beaming.

"And take your sister!" said his mother.

Khaled quickly, but carefully, closed the book of Pliny, slid it into a leather satchel, and hid the satchel under the rug where he slept. Then he grabbed his sister, who was shouting "Lubna oony-corn!" Which meant, "Lubna wants to go see the unicorns!"

Khaled arrived at the main road to find most of the town milling around awaiting the arrival of the unicorns.

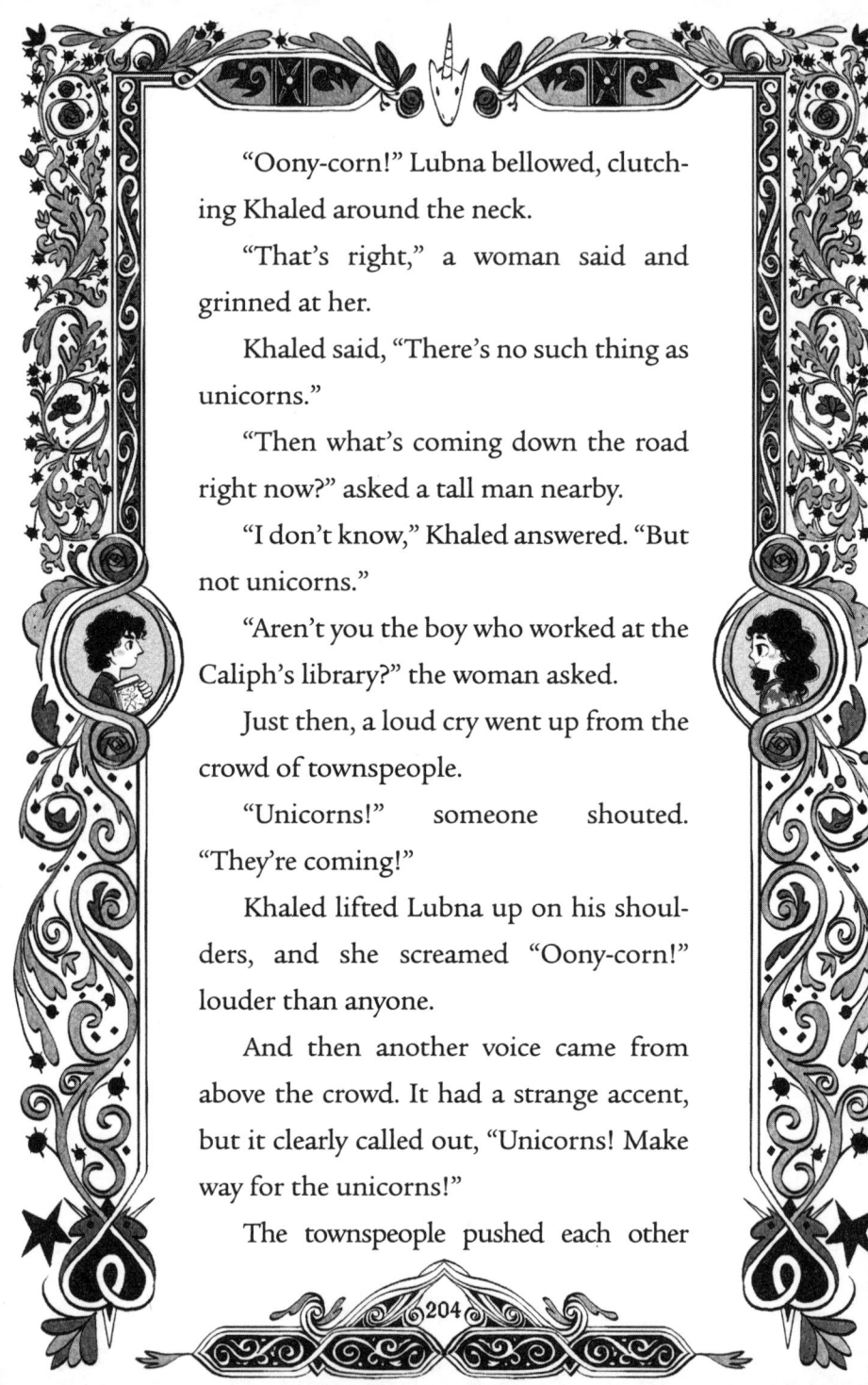

"Oony-corn!" Lubna bellowed, clutching Khaled around the neck.

"That's right," a woman said and grinned at her.

Khaled said, "There's no such thing as unicorns."

"Then what's coming down the road right now?" asked a tall man nearby.

"I don't know," Khaled answered. "But not unicorns."

"Aren't you the boy who worked at the Caliph's library?" the woman asked.

Just then, a loud cry went up from the crowd of townspeople.

"Unicorns!" someone shouted. "They're coming!"

Khaled lifted Lubna up on his shoulders, and she screamed "Oony-corn!" louder than anyone.

And then another voice came from above the crowd. It had a strange accent, but it clearly called out, "Unicorns! Make way for the unicorns!"

The townspeople pushed each other

backward, out of the roadway. Above their heads, Khaled saw the source of the strange voice. It was a man, wearing the mysterious black robes of a Christian monk, crying out "Unicorn!" in Khaled's language. And he was bobbing up and down—on the back of a unicorn. A girl with eyes as green as a leaf, and a boy who looked like he was probably her brother, rode unicorns behind the monk.

"Oony-corn!" Lubna shrieked, smacking Khaled's head with both her palms in excitement.

"Ow! Ow! Stop, Lubna!" Khaled laughed. And he strained to see over the fully grown men and women who were all standing on their toes to get a glimpse of the unicorns.

There appeared to be hundreds of them. Khaled gazed at the unicorns. He couldn't *believe* they were *real*. And that he was *seeing* them.

And as they came even with him at last, Khaled *really* couldn't believe it.

Because they were clearly *not* unicorns.

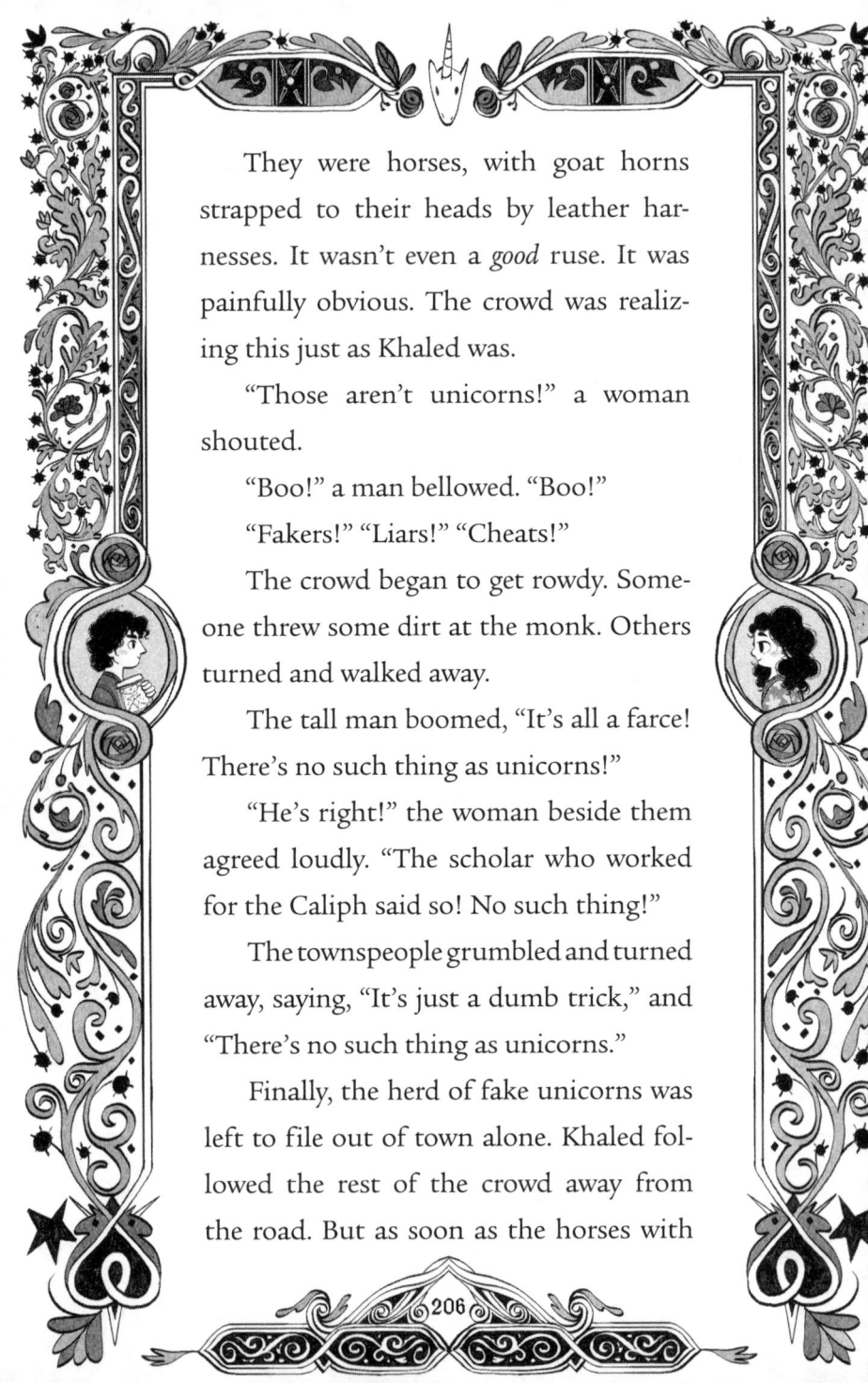

They were horses, with goat horns strapped to their heads by leather harnesses. It wasn't even a *good* ruse. It was painfully obvious. The crowd was realizing this just as Khaled was.

"Those aren't unicorns!" a woman shouted.

"Boo!" a man bellowed. "Boo!"

"Fakers!" "Liars!" "Cheats!"

The crowd began to get rowdy. Someone threw some dirt at the monk. Others turned and walked away.

The tall man boomed, "It's all a farce! There's no such thing as unicorns!"

"He's right!" the woman beside them agreed loudly. "The scholar who worked for the Caliph said so! No such thing!"

The townspeople grumbled and turned away, saying, "It's just a dumb trick," and "There's no such thing as unicorns."

Finally, the herd of fake unicorns was left to file out of town alone. Khaled followed the rest of the crowd away from the road. But as soon as the horses with

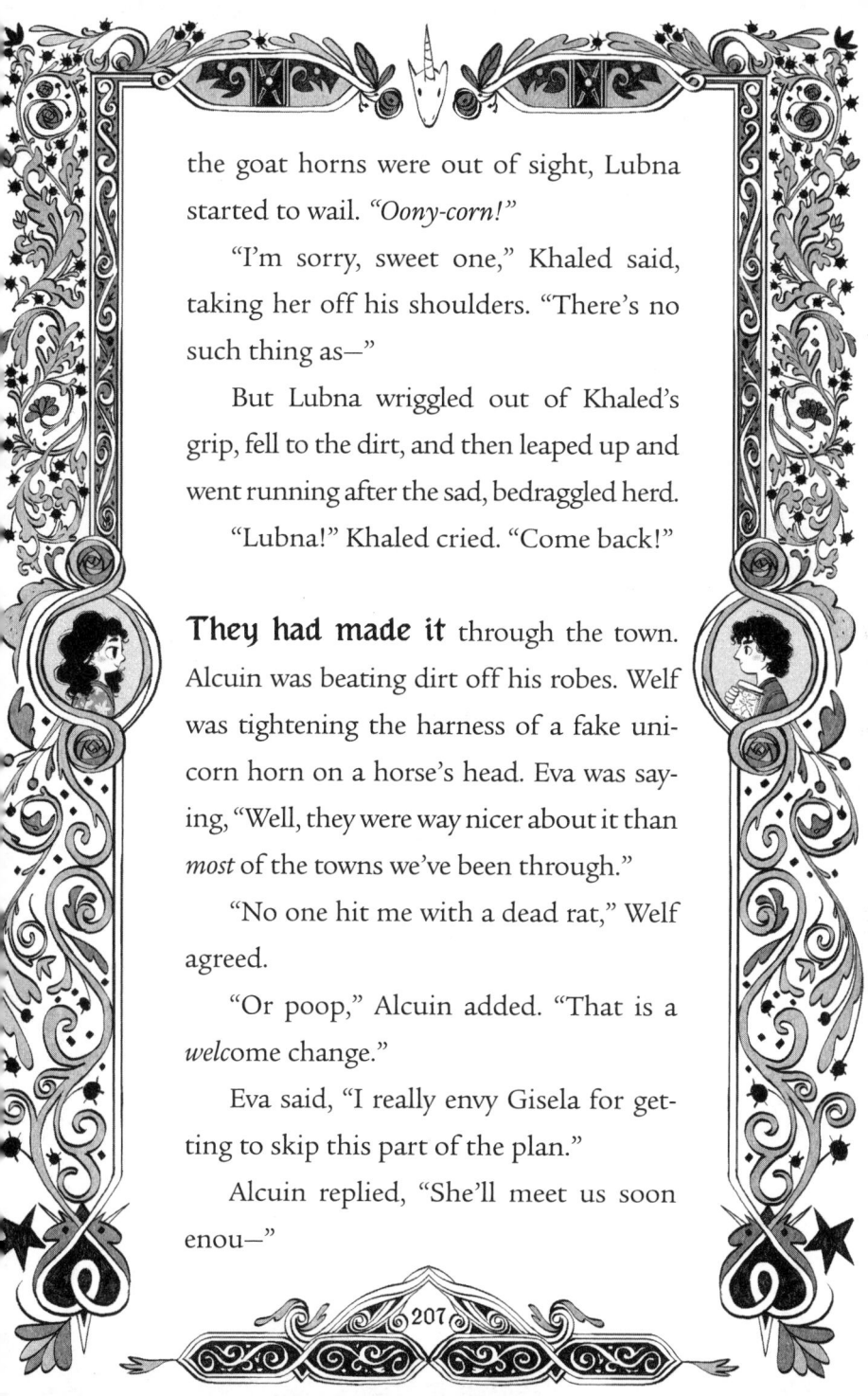

the goat horns were out of sight, Lubna started to wail. *"Oony-corn!"*

"I'm sorry, sweet one," Khaled said, taking her off his shoulders. "There's no such thing as—"

But Lubna wriggled out of Khaled's grip, fell to the dirt, and then leaped up and went running after the sad, bedraggled herd.

"Lubna!" Khaled cried. "Come back!"

They had made it through the town. Alcuin was beating dirt off his robes. Welf was tightening the harness of a fake unicorn horn on a horse's head. Eva was saying, "Well, they were way nicer about it than *most* of the towns we've been through."

"No one hit me with a dead rat," Welf agreed.

"Or poop," Alcuin added. "That is a *welc*ome change."

Eva said, "I really envy Gisela for getting to skip this part of the plan."

Alcuin replied, "She'll meet us soon enou—"

"Oony-corn! Oony-corn!"

They spun toward the source of the sound. An adorable little girl, no older than two, was barreling toward them down the road, her black curls bouncing with every step, her tiny arms spread wide. A teenage boy was running after her and calling, "Lubna!"

But the girl was surprisingly fast. She ran right into the herd of horses, amongst their legs.

"Stop her!" Alcuin shouted. Eva and Welf were already running, trying to scoop up the girl before she was kicked or trampled.

The big boy plunged into the herd after his sister.

Khaled found Lubna at the same moment as the girl with the leaf-green eyes did. He scooped Lubna up, but the little girl reached out and stroked the gray flank of a huge beast with her tiny fingers, cooing, *"Oony-corn...."* Her face was perfectly blissful.

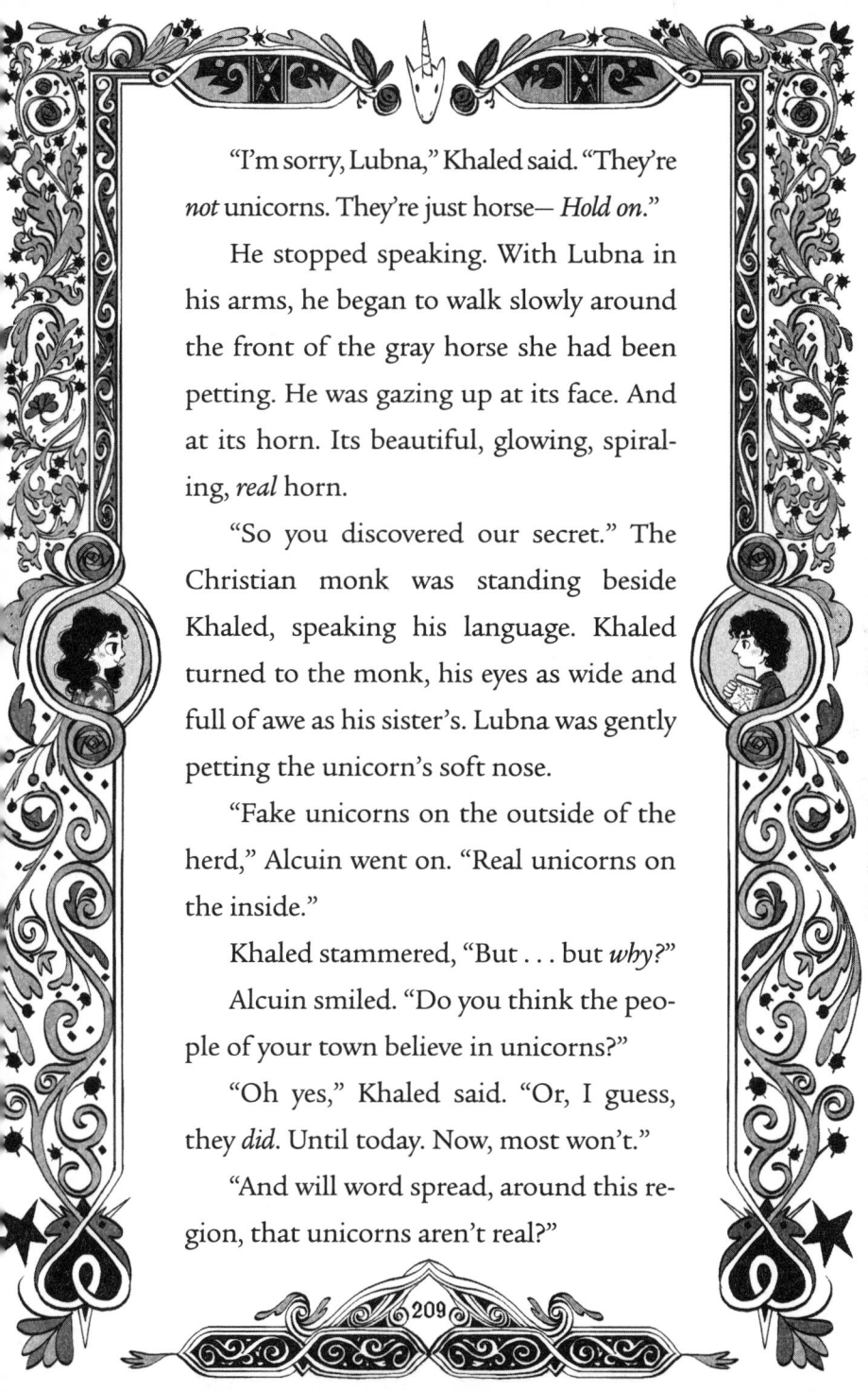

"I'm sorry, Lubna," Khaled said. "They're *not* unicorns. They're just horse— *Hold on*."

He stopped speaking. With Lubna in his arms, he began to walk slowly around the front of the gray horse she had been petting. He was gazing up at its face. And at its horn. Its beautiful, glowing, spiraling, *real* horn.

"So you discovered our secret." The Christian monk was standing beside Khaled, speaking his language. Khaled turned to the monk, his eyes as wide and full of awe as his sister's. Lubna was gently petting the unicorn's soft nose.

"Fake unicorns on the outside of the herd," Alcuin went on. "Real unicorns on the inside."

Khaled stammered, "But . . . but *why?*"

Alcuin smiled. "Do you think the people of your town believe in unicorns?"

"Oh yes," Khaled said. "Or, I guess, they *did*. Until today. Now, most won't."

"And will word spread, around this region, that unicorns aren't real?"

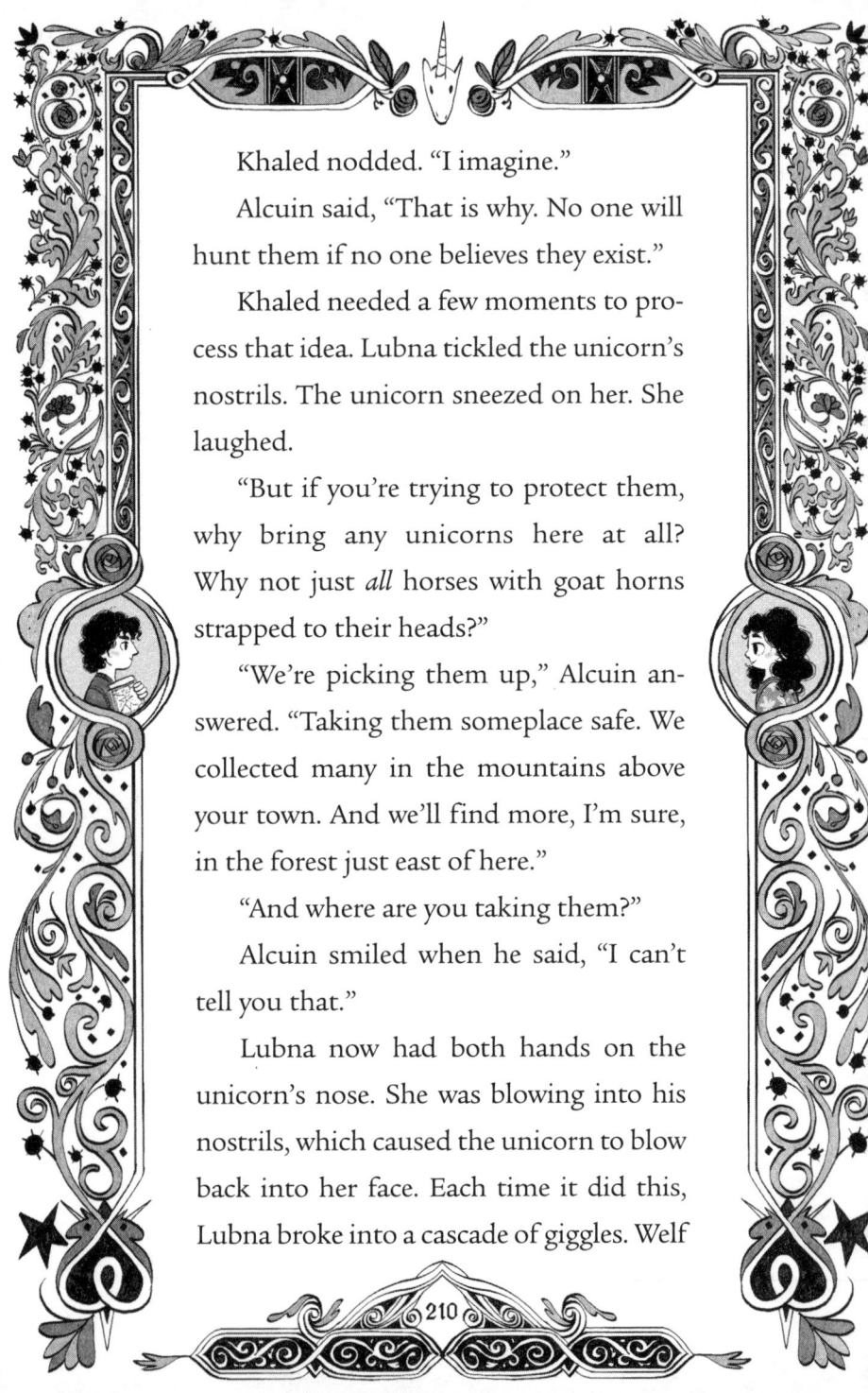

Khaled nodded. "I imagine."

Alcuin said, "That is why. No one will hunt them if no one believes they exist."

Khaled needed a few moments to process that idea. Lubna tickled the unicorn's nostrils. The unicorn sneezed on her. She laughed.

"But if you're trying to protect them, why bring any unicorns here at all? Why not just *all* horses with goat horns strapped to their heads?"

"We're picking them up," Alcuin answered. "Taking them someplace safe. We collected many in the mountains above your town. And we'll find more, I'm sure, in the forest just east of here."

"And where are you taking them?"

Alcuin smiled when he said, "I can't tell you that."

Lubna now had both hands on the unicorn's nose. She was blowing into his nostrils, which caused the unicorn to blow back into her face. Each time it did this, Lubna broke into a cascade of giggles. Welf and Eva, who couldn't understand anything Alcuin and Khaled said, were watching Lubna and laughing along with her.

Alcuin asked Khaled about himself. Khaled explained that he was a scholar-in-training for the Caliph. Studying Pliny. Learning of the creatures of the world.

Alcuin said, "We could use someone like you."

Suddenly suspicious, Khaled asked, "Who is 'we'?"

Alcuin gestured at Eva and Welf. "We are the Secret Order of the Unicorn." And then he added, "Join us. We could use a member here in Córdoba."

Lubna shrieked joyfully as the unicorn blew her curly hair back from her face with another blast from his nostrils.

Khaled glanced at his sister. He took a deep breath. And then he said, "Could you use *two*?"

TO BE CONTINUED . . .

ACKNOWLEDGMENTS

FIRST AND MOST IMPORTANTLY, we would like to thank the people of Laredo, Texas. Both David and Adam have visited Laredo a number of times, and there are few cities on the planet where the people are more welcoming and warm.

Adam was first invited to visit Laredo years ago by Laura Gonzalez-Ortiz, teacher extraordinaire at George Washington Middle School. He told Grimm fairy tales to just about every middle school student in the district, and they laughed and screamed and only heckled him a little bit. The first time Adam ever got a book on the bestseller list, it was because of the kids, and parents, and teachers, and librarians, and booksellers of Laredo.

A special shout-out is due to the young writers of the Writer's Block of Laredo, a group of students Adam and David worked with, who gave them a number of ideas for this book.

ADAM WOULD ALSO LIKE TO THANK David Bowles—a resident of the Río Grande Valley, a scholar of Mesoamerican mythology and border lore, a brilliant and award-winning writer, and a truly good dude.

DAVID WOULD ALSO LIKE TO THANK his real-life community—Mexicans and Mexican Americans on both sides of the river—and his virtual family, Latinx writers of kid lit throughout the hemisphere. *Juntos podemos con todo.*

PHOTO CREDIT: UTRGV

David Bowles is a Mexican American author from the very tip of Texas, a sleepy little border town called Donna. His childhood was filled with the magical tales of his grandmother, Marie Garza, who encouraged David to read. Because of his family's roots in Mexico, he has traveled all over that country, visiting the ruins of ancient cities, studying native folklore, indigenous languages, and tales of strange creatures like the chupacabras. He is also a college professor whose goal is to be as eccentric as Mito Fauna in a few years. Among his books are the Pura Belpré Honor–winning *The Smoking Mirror* and *They Call Me Güero*.

WRITING ABOUT THE BORDER brings me a lot of joy, but also some worry. This is my community, full of my people—relatives and friends on both sides of the river. Our lives overflow with two cultures, two languages, two national identities. Trust me. You'd love it here.

But it's easy for people to misunderstand what they're not familiar with, so this book had to be not just about an amazing adventure in South Texas, but also about how easy it is for outsiders to get the wrong impression of my community. Heck, even those of us *living* down here don't always agree about how this side of the border and that one fit together.

We couldn't just pretend that some people aren't nervous about the border. We also couldn't ignore the fact that many border folks don't like the choices the government is making.

So Adam and I decided to include that disagreement in the book. We know people who feel both ways about the barrier that's been going up along the border in bits and pieces for years now. It was important to get a good look at those two sides without assuming that either group wants to hurt anyone.

As a Mexican American, I also wanted to make sure that the bilingual and bicultural nature of my people came through loud and clear. I am proud of my heritage, my roots along either bank of the Río Grande. And that also meant taking the *chupacabras*—pretty recent cryptids in the long history of creepy creatures in South Texas—and finding where they fit into the larger indigenous mythology of our ancestors.

I can only hope that the low whistling I hear drifting over the water as I write these words is a sign of their approval.

— *D.B.*

PHOTO CREDIT: Lauren Mancia

Adam Gidwitz taught big kids and not-so-big kids in Brooklyn for eight years. Now he spends most of his time chronicling the adventures of the Unicorn Rescue Society. He is also the author of the Newbery Honor–winning *The Inquisitor's Tale,* as well as the bestselling *A Tale Dark and Grimm* and its companions. He is also the creator of the podcast *Grimmest.*

PHOTO CREDIT: Amy Cao

Jesse Casey and **Chris Lenox Smith** are filmmakers. They founded Mixtape Club, an award-winning production company in New York City, where they make videos and animations for all sorts of people.

Adam and Jesse met when they were eleven years old. They have done many things together, like building a car powered only by a mousetrap and inventing two board games. Jesse and Chris met when they were eighteen years old. They have done many things together, too, like making music videos for rock bands and an animation for the largest digital billboard ever. But Adam and Jesse and Chris wanted to do something *together*. First, they made trailers for Adam's books. Then, they made a short film together. And now, they are sharing with the world the courage, curiosity, kindness, and courage of the members of the Unicorn Rescue Society!

Hatem Aly is an Egyptian-born illustrator whose work has been featured in multiple publications worldwide. He currently lives in beautiful New Brunswick, Canada, with his wife, son, and more pets than people. His illustrated work

includes the Newbery Honor winner *The Inquisitor's Tale* by Adam Gidwitz, the Unicorn Rescue Society series also by Adam Gidwitz with several amazing contributing authors, the Story Pirates book series with Geoff Rodkey and Jacqueline West, early readers series Meet Yasmin with Saadia Faruqi, and *How to Feed Your Parents* by Ryan Miller. He has more upcoming books and projects in the works. You can find him online @metahatem.